Buenos Aires D

Finding the prescription for a love that lasts...

Meet the dedicated medics of the Hospital General de Buenos Aires. They might be winners in their work, but they all need a little help when it comes to finding their happy-ever-afters!

Luckily for them, passion is sweeping through the corridors of the hospital like a virus and no one is immune! Are they brave enough to take their chance on happiness...and each other?

Find out in

Sebastián and Isabella's story
ER Doc's Miracle Triplets by Tina Beckett

Carlos and Sofia's story
Surgeon's Brooding Brazilian Rival by Luana DaRosa

Available now!

Gabriel and Ana's story
Daring to Fall for the Single Dad by Becky Wicks

Felipe and Emilia's story
Secretly Dating the Baby Doc by JC Harroway

Coming next month!

Dear Reader,

Surgeon's Brooding Brazilian Rival really was a team effort. I loved the idea of four interconnected stories taking place in the same hospital from the moment it was pitched—and I'm really happy to welcome you to Sofia and Carlos's story.

You have yet to dive into the story, but a central part of it is Carlos's anxiety and how it affects his work. Anxiety is a constant companion in my own life, and so getting to talk about mental health in the context of the hero in this story was a great privilege.

I hope you enjoy reading it as much as I enjoyed writing it!

Luana <3

SURGEON'S BROODING BRAZILIAN RIVAL

LUANA DaROSA

Harlequin

MEDICAL ROMANCE

Special thanks and acknowledgment are given to Luana DaRosa for her contribution to the Buenos Aires Docs miniseries.

Harlequin®
MEDICAL ROMANCE

Recycling programs for this product may not exist in your area.

ISBN-13: 978-1-335-59553-9

Surgeon's Brooding Brazilian Rival

Harlequin Enterprises ULC
22 Adelaide St. West, 41st Floor
Toronto, Ontario M5H 4E3, Canada
www.Harlequin.com

Printed in U.S.A.

Once at home in sunny Brazil, **Luana DaRosa** has since lived on three different continents, though her favorite romantic location remains the tropical places of Latin America. When she's not typing away at her latest romance novel or reading about love, Luana is either crocheting, buying yarn she doesn't need or chasing her bunnies around her house. She lives with her partner in a cozy town in the south of England. Find her on Twitter under the handle @ludarosabooks.

Books by Luana DaRosa

Harlequin Medical Romance

Amazon River Vets

The Vet's Convenient Bride
The Secret She Kept from Dr. Delgado

Falling for Her Off-Limits Boss
Her Secret Rio Baby
Falling Again for the Brazilian Doc
A Therapy Pup to Reunite Them

Visit the Author Profile page at Harlequin.com.

For my sister Lorena, beschti schwöstr für ewig

CHAPTER ONE

THE SOUND OF water pouring out of the tap and skin rubbing against skin filled the scrub room. Carlos looked up from the sink, his eyes scanning the operating room through the window. The members of staff stood by their assigned places, waiting for their patient to be brought in. A patient that should have already been here five minutes ago when the ER had paged him to let him know an emergency surgery was coming up.

His eyes narrowed on the clock on the other side of the OR, and his lips pressed into a thin line as he watched the seconds tick by. He released the foot pedal, and the flow of water stopped. When he turned around, the OR nurse was already waiting with a towel for him to dry his arms before helping him into the gown and gloves.

'Where is our patient?' Carlos asked as he stepped through the doors.

'I'll call them to find out,' one nurse said, and Carlos nodded as she approached the phone hanging on the wall next to the monitoring equipment. As he waited, he let his eyes wander around the room, giving each staff member a once-over. The surgeon assisting him was missing, too. They were most likely with the patient transport after having done the initial consult.

He'd arrived at Hospital General de Buenos Aires almost a week ago. *This* was the first time the staff hadn't impressed him with the level of service and dedication they put forward. Sebastián Lopez, the joint head of emergency medicine at the hospital with his wife, Isabella, had approached him at a conference where Carlos had been one of the keynote speakers.

Though they had mainly spoken about Carlos's specific method of triaging during a multidiscipline surgery, he'd got the feeling from the other man that there had been more to the conversation. That 'more' turned out to be a job offer to come to Buenos Aires and teach the trauma surgeons there how to run a service the way Carlos Cabrera would.

This was definitely not how Carlos Cabrera ran his trauma surgery. In his world, early was on time, and on time was already being late. Which made this patient transport *very* late. In his discipline of medicine, every second counted, and he'd witnessed enough cases where those few extra seconds had decided between life and death.

For a member of *his* team to be late in delivering a patient was unacceptable. The ER was right underneath the trauma surgery ORs. He knew exactly how long it took for a patient to be transported upstairs because on his first day he'd timed it himself, so he knew what to expect from the people on the team.

Carlos rolled his jaw, forcing the tight muscles to relax when the doors finally opened and the gurney with the patient rolled into the OR.

'Get into gear, everyone. Time's wasting,' Carlos said, turning towards the anaesthetist with an impatient nod.

'There was a—' a female voice said behind him, but he cut her off without turning around.

'I'm not interested in excuses, only that we start this surgery with no further delay. Are you my missing surgeon?' He watched the anaesthetist remove the IV drip from the patient's arm and insert the cannula to push the anaesthetic through.

'I'm *a* trauma surgeon at this hospital, but I'm certainly not *your* surgeon.' Carlos furrowed his brow and looked over his shoulder as the woman spoke in clipped words. What was that supposed to mean? But all he caught was a wisp of brown hair that vanished behind the door to the scrub room.

His eyes shot to the window where the woman appeared a heartbeat later, her lips moving in a silent litany as she stuck her hands under the tap. Their gazes collided when she looked up, and a strange sensation of familiarity washed over him as he beheld the honey-brown eyes. Sebastián had introduced Carlos to all the surgeons on staff when he had arrived earlier in the week, including her.

Her smile had been wide as she greeted him, her grip strong when she shook his hand, and the scent of apricot had lingered in his nose long after he'd turned to other staff members to greet them. It was that scent that came rushing into his conscious mind now, setting his focus off-kilter.

Carlos's hand had lingered on hers for a fraction of a second, enough time for a spark to travel up his arm and spread an unfamiliar heat through his chest. It was the echo of that heat rising inside of him again that kept his eyes glued to her face, watching her through the glass.

'The patient had a tracheotomy performed. I'll connect the tube to the ventilator, and we'll have to switch to manual aspiration once you're ready to pull it out,' the anaesthetist said behind him, forcing Carlos out of his head and back into the OR.

'A tracheotomy?' He spun around to face the patient, stepping closer and bending down to inspect the tube sticking out of his patient's throat.

The briefing he'd received just ten minutes ago

didn't include any information about a blocked airway that required this form of intubation. A part of him wanted to turn around again and face the woman—Dr Martinez, Sebastián's voice echoed in his head—to ask her what had happened. But the loud beeping of a monitor drew his attention back to the critical condition of his patient.

'His blood pressure is dropping. We need to get him open now and take care of the internal bleeding.' Pushing the swirl of thoughts away, Carlos stepped towards the patient and reached his hand out to receive the scalpel the OR nurse already held in her hand.

'This is not good,' Carlos mumbled to himself as he opened the patient up and beheld the extent of the injury.

Though he had worked in trauma surgery from the moment he had started his internship in Rio de Janeiro many years ago, seeing some of the devastation the human body could withstand didn't get any less humbling—especially when he was the one knitting people back together.

'I need an extra pair of hands,' he said, and as he was about to look up to search for Dr Martinez, two slender gloved hands appeared in his field of vision.

'I'm here,' she said, not offering any other comment about her lateness. Not that it mattered. He had meant it when he said he wasn't interested in what had taken her so long. They could have that argument later.

'Nice of you to join us, Martinez,' he said, unable to help himself with the jab. In all his years working at the largest emergency rooms all across South America, he hadn't let a single co-surgeon down, and it was that kind of dedication he expected from everyone else.

Her eyes shot up at him and narrowed into slits, and for a distracting second, he wondered what her lips looked like underneath her mask. Were they drawn into a tight line, hiding their fullness from view?

'Blood is pooling around the liver, and there's a discolouration of his kidney. Something to look at once we get the bleeding under control.' Carlos focused his mind on the surgery at hand, a frown tugging at the corners of his lips as he realised how easily Dr Martinez held his attention.

What was it about her that drew him in without his permission? He hadn't even spent any time with her outside of their brief introduction.

'Suction or sponges?' Martinez asked, her hand already outstretched to grasp whatever he said.

'I'll take suction while you pack the liver and stop more blood from pooling,' he replied, and took the aspirator from the nurse.

The sputtering of the suction drowned out the

beeping of the monitor, and Carlos listened to the anaesthetist keeping him appraised of the vital signs of the patient.

'The ER said he was in an accident on a construction site. Do you know what happened?' He didn't look up as he asked the question, his hand steady as he cleared the surgical field of the excess blood. 'Hand me the stapler, please,' he said as he handed the suction tube off.

'You're going to staple the laceration shut?' That question was the first thing Dr Martinez had said since she had begun packing the liver and its surroundings with surgical sponges to soak up as much blood as possible. With her efforts on these fronts and him suctioning the rest away, he could now see where the organ had torn on impact.

'Staples are quicker than sutures and just as effective,' he countered, then placed the medical stapler onto the cut and set the first staple. 'There will be some scarring, but considering the situation he's in, it will be the least of his problems.'

Carlos didn't wait for Dr Martinez to object any further and stapled the rest of the wound with sure, swift hands.

'He got crushed underneath a steel beam,' she said when he had finished closing the cut on the liver, and it took Carlos a second to remember the context. He'd asked what had happened.

'The bruising on the kidney worries me. Not

enough to put in a drain, though… He's hanging on right now, but the thread is thin. There will be follow-up surgeries in the next few days.' Carlos paused, assessing the patient before going over to the monitor with the vital signs on it. The patient's blood pressure had evened out, showing Carlos they had stopped the source of the internal bleeding.

'With an injury like this, he could suffer from crush syndrome. If he's stable enough to be transported, we should put him on fluids and monitor his kidney function every hour,' Dr Martinez said, to which Carlos nodded.

'Very well, Martinez. Let's close him up.'

The rest of the surgery went by without another hitch, and Sofia was grateful for that. Her hands were steady, but her breath quickened and came out in short, quick bursts.

I'm not interested in any excuses.

His words echoed in her head throughout the surgery, sending waves of hot and cold through her. The last time she'd received such a dressing down had been during her internship years ago from a particularly difficult senior surgeon. Carlos Cabrera was apparently trying to rival him as the most unpleasant surgeon she'd ever had the misfortune to work with.

Dr Morales had never passed up an opportunity

to criticise her in front of her peers, taking any excuse to reprimand her. What exactly made her that special to the old surgeon, she never knew. But because of his scathing words, Sofia got into the habit of triple-checking every single step inside and outside of the OR. The rule book had become her best friend because her only defence had been to explain her actions in the context of medical studies and guides.

Unlike the grumpy surgeon from her internship, at least Carlos was easy on the eyes when he gave her grief. His cheekbones were set high, the gentle slope downward giving his face a regal quality that was both alluring and infuriatingly superior. Along with the perfectly groomed hair and brown eyes that seemed to note everything around them, he resembled an actor playing a surgeon. The impression had been so stark, Sofia couldn't help but stare, inexplicably drawn to him.

Sebastián himself had told her he and the chief of surgery had worked together to bring Carlos here. They wanted the entire surgical and emergency medicine team to learn from him.

And the worst part about the surgery today was that she actually *had* learned something. Staples weren't a new invention, and she had used them plenty of times when working in the emergency room to quickly patch up surface wounds. But for repairing damage she found internally, Sofia always took the time to do the sutures, sometimes even feeling hurried during high-pressure situations.

Staples were a quick and easy solution, the downside of them being excessive scarring that could lead to further complications. But in a discipline like trauma surgery, the quick fix was most often also the right fix.

The heart rate monitor beeped, drawing Sofia's thoughts back into the OR as Alejandra, the junior surgeon next to her, shuffled her feet. Alejandra's surgical gown rustled as she bent over the patient to look at his throat.

'Are we leaving the tracheotomy like this?' Alejandra asked.

'Yes,' Carlos replied just as Sofia had finished taking a breath to answer the question herself. 'In the state he's in, he'll need to remain intubated and on ventilation. There will be a follow-up surgery tomorrow where the cardiovascular team will decide what to do.'

Alejandra nodded, and Sofia bit back a sharp retort and forced her hand to relax. As he spoke, her grip around the retractor had tightened.

Why was she so bothered by this guy? He wasn't *that* special. Although she couldn't deny the admiration she felt—much like the look she saw on Alejandra's face. She recognised his potential to teach her much, and her skin flushed every time she looked at him, reminded of the expertise he brought to the table.

When he was working opposite her in the OR, it was far too easy to get lost in his lilting baritone voice as he narrated the surgery while her eyes tracked his every more.

Now as he patted the film dressing on the incision wound onto the patient's skin. His fingers moved with an unexpected delicacy, contrasting with his stern demeanour. The soft touch evoked an unbidden thought in the back of her mind as Sofia wondered what his hands would feel like without the gloves. Would they feel rough as each of his calluses scraped against her skin?

'You ready for the tape, Martinez?' His deep voice dragged her out of the fantasy playing in her head, and Sofia repressed a shudder. Carlos touching her was not only inappropriate, it was also *not* how she felt about him. Wherever that thought had come from, it needed to go straight back there and never return.

'Yes, of course,' she said, swallowing the *sorry* that was forming on her tongue. She might have been more apologetic to other colleagues, but if Carlos wanted to be abrasive, then he could take it as well.

Pulling the tape to the appropriate size, she held it out to Alejandra, who cut it. Then she angled the piece of tape to align with where Carlos's hand was holding down the dressing. She placed it at the far end, patting it so it would stick, and then slowly ran her hand up the dressing, flattening the tape until her hand connected with Carlos's, which was still holding the film in place.

The spark created by that small touch travelled down her arm in an electric wave, singeing everything in its wake. The sensation took her by surprise, her lips parting as a soft, unbidden gasp emerged.

An instant later, his eyes shot up to hers, narrowed into slits as he levelled a stare at her. Dear God, had he heard her even over the low whirring of the ventilator and the constant beeping from the vital monitors? The last thing she needed was Carlos Cabrera thinking she had a thing for him.

'You're assigned to my operating room for today?' Carlos asked as he turned away to let the nurse assist him with his gown. Sofia noted the terse undertone in his voice. He had *definitely* caught her gasp.

'I am. Is that going to be a problem?' she asked curtly, even though she knew she shouldn't, and turned as well to get help with her own surgical gown.

After the public dressing down he'd given her about being late, she didn't care. What would have the other option been? Not performing a tracheotomy on the patient? She would have been on time, but there wouldn't have been a need for surgery at all.

When Carlos didn't answer, she whirled around to look at him and caught a glimpse of an amused expression before the shutters fell down, leaving her with nothing but the mask of cool professionalism she already knew he usually wore.

'Just don't be late again and we won't have any problems,' he said before turning towards the anaesthetist, trying to get his attention.

As he turned away, a sinking feeling settled in her stomach. An entire afternoon with him? She sighed, mentally bracing herself. He'd better not make any other big deals about her conduct. Sofia was not about to withhold any life-saving measures just because he liked to keep to the schedule. Surgery was unpredictable, and she'd thought a renowned surgeon like Carlos would have understood that better.

CHAPTER TWO

THE REST OF her afternoon went by uneventfully, and Sofia had avoided any further accidental contact or any meaningful conversation with Carlos. Something that she was now, one day later, making an ironclad rule. She would listen to him whenever he conducted the staff training to learn whatever she could without getting too close.

Sofia also didn't have any issues performing surgeries with him—quite the opposite. Despite his abrasiveness, their rhythm in the OR matched each other's, like the same people had taught them how to operate, and despite her discontent with him, she had to admit that they worked well as a surgical unit.

Though she didn't want to give him too much credit for that. With the amount of praise he received from the medical community, he should be able to work with anyone and adapt to their style. Was that what had happened with them? He'd picked up on her personal style and modelled his own after it?

The thought of Carlos observing her so closely brought a flush to her cheeks, and a warm surge rose from her neck to her forehead. What else had he seen while he had his eye on her? Had he noticed how much attention she'd paid him? How impressed she had been with his skill despite not wanting to? She had promised herself she would not fall for this squeaky-clean façade Carlos Cabrera was putting on. Okay, maybe he was handsome and talented and hard-working, but that didn't mean he deserved the special treatment everyone was giving him—including Sebastián.

Sofia's eyes narrowed as the head of emergency medicine walked towards the nurses' station where she was finishing up her patient notes from a surgery earlier. The hum of the ER was a familiar backdrop as she worked, undisturbed by the rattling of stretchers transporting patients and the beeping of pagers.

'Hablando del Rey de Roma...' she said, raising her voice above the noise drifting towards them from the trauma bays as he came towards her with an unmistakable swagger in his step. 'What has you so bouncy this morning?'

Sebastián laughed at that, coming to a halt next to her and leaning his elbow on the counter. 'Love, my friend. It's the best thing out there to elevate your mood. You should try it.'

Sofia snorted at that, but the breath caught in her throat as the unbidden image of Carlos flashed through her mind again, his fingers sure and nimble as he'd stapled shut the wound on their shared patient. Whatever qualms she had, she couldn't deny his skills as a surgeon.

Sebastián noticed the hesitation she tried to mask as a cough and tilted his head to the side in a silent question. A question Sofia had no intention of answering. Love might have worked for her chief, but it definitely wasn't for her. Surgery was a very competitive field, trauma surgery even more so.

Sofia sighed. 'You know how it is out there. No one understands what it's like to be in a relationship with a surgeon until I've cancelled five dates in a row. They somehow seem to think my day ends at 5:00 p.m., regardless of whether I'm elbow-deep in someone's chest cavity.'

Every single boyfriend of hers had claimed to understand that her job needed to come first—until they didn't, leaving her to pick up the pieces. Again.

Sebastián raised his hands in front of him. 'I know you struggled, especially with that one guy. David?'

'Daniel,' Sofia said, the name twisting something deep inside her gut.

Once she had thought she'd found someone

who understood that work would always be her
first responsibility. But Daniel had turned out to
be the worst of all of them. The other men in her
life had at least had the decency to tell her that
things hadn't been working out for them. Daniel
had cheated on her, then blamed her dedication
to work for his missteps. The words still burned
a hole in her heart whenever she recalled them.

'Daniel, right…' Sebastián shook his head, no
doubt recalling the mess Daniel had left behind
when they'd broken up. Though it reminded her of
the one good thing that had come out of the mess
of their relationship. She and Isabella had grown
much closer as the other woman had helped her
put the pieces of her life back together.

'How is Isabella doing?' Sofia asked, pushing
away the storm of emotions bubbling up within
her whenever she thought about her ex and focus-
ing on her friendship with the husband-and-wife
team leading the OR.

'She's good. So are the triplets. Her doctors
have asked her to take it easy, but you know how
she is. Even when she's not at the hospital, I find
her at home repainting the nursery for the sev-
enth time or cleaning out the garage.'

He rolled his eyes in exasperation, but she
could see the playfulness behind his words—
along with the genuine worry that his wife was
overdoing it.

Sebastián and Isabella Lopez had taken charge of the ER in the Hospital General de Buenos Aires many years ago and transformed it from an underperforming emergency room to the renowned trauma centre it was now. Though Sofia hadn't been there then—she'd only started working here three years ago—she'd heard enough from other staff about the transformation of the hospital.

'That sounds like Bella,' she said with a chuckle, and a familiar warmth spread through her chest at the thought of the other woman. 'You know she won't slow down until she's too pregnant to move.'

Sebastián sighed, shaking his head. 'I've been keeping her busy with administrative things to do around the hospital. But I'm actually running out of things to distract her with.' He paused, then mumbled more to himself than Sofia, 'Maybe I should send her to Cabrera. They can document his trainings together.'

The mention of Carlos changed the comfortable warmth inside her to a searing heat, the biting flames emerging at the mention of his name. Flames of annoyance, Sofia told herself as her spine stiffened.

'I meant to talk to you about him and why the hell senior leadership thought he was a necessary addition to the team,' she said, releasing those feelings in a channelled burst towards the person who was partially responsible for Carlos Cabrera being here.

Sebastián's eyebrows rose all the way to his hairline. 'You don't like him?' His tone had a fragile edge to it, as if her words had genuinely saddened him.

'Oh, God, are you under his spell, too? What is wrong with everyone?' Sofia raised her hands in disbelief when Sebastián's face remained puzzled. 'He's a decent surgeon, but there isn't much more to him. What's with the obsession?'

'Is…there a problem I should know about?' She noticed a slight shift in his tone, one she recognised as his 'boss' voice, and she shook her head. Though Sofia had a few choice words to say about Carlos, she knew she wasn't in the right frame of mind to let it out constructively. Sebastián wasn't technically leading the surgical department, but she spent so much time in the ER that they had become close enough to share their opinions with each other. He had even helped her out with proposals for senior leadership, including himself.

'I just think he's a bit…arrogant,' she said, which was part of the truth she wanted to tell Sebastián—when the time was right.

Sebastián chuckled at that. 'I see the professional rivalry is already in full swing. Don't get too wrapped up in this, Sofia. He's here on a one-month contract, and then he'll be off to the next place.'

Her ears perked up at that. 'You don't want him here permanently?'

'Oh, no, believe me, I do. *He* doesn't want a full-time position here. Cabrera hasn't stayed at a place for more than six months for the last five years, and neither I nor the chief of surgery could change his mind.'

Sofia furrowed her brow at that. 'He's been travelling around to different hospitals for the last five years. Why?'

'No idea, but we can ask him together,' Sebastián said as he pointed with his chin to a spot behind her.

Her head whipped around, her eyes widening as she saw the subject of their conversation walk towards them. His head was tilted downwards, and the line between his eyebrows was getting progressively deeper at whatever he was looking at on his phone. He hadn't seen her, had he?

Sofia hesitated as different paths opened up in her mind. The last thing she wanted was to give him the satisfaction of running away from him, dodging wayward stretchers and scurrying colleagues in the process. But she was in no mood for being in his presence any longer than she needed to—and that included unscheduled run-ins in the ER. Everything about him was too much. His attitude, the skill he wasn't shy of flaunting, his subtle scent of pine that kept drifting up her nose whenever she crossed paths with him and brought a tingling sensation to her fingertips whenever she closed her eyes…

'I should go,' she said when the spark she had just been thinking about travelled down her arms again, and didn't give the Sebastián the time to say anything in return before speed-walking to the next door in sight and vanishing behind it.

'Cabrera.' Carlos looked up and glimpsed the grey scrubs the trauma team wore vanishing behind the door to a supply closet. It slammed shut just as he stopped in front of Sebastián Lopez, who had been the one to call his name.

'Lopez, good to see you,' he said to the head of the ER. He wasn't necessarily sure what they had to talk about, but his professional courtesy didn't let him walk past one of his superiors— especially not when he'd called on him by name. 'What can I do for you?'

Something flickered over the expression of the other man, a feeling he couldn't quite pin down. Annoyance? Carlos raised his eyes to the door that had just slammed shut a few seconds ago, and Sebastián followed his gaze with a sigh. He opened his mouth to say something when the pager hanging from his waistband went off. He glanced at it, then frowned and stood up straight.

'The chief of medicine is asking for me. Listen…' Sebastián shot another glance at the door and then shrugged. 'Don't worry, there was bound to be friction, but she'll come around. Just keep on teaching everyone like we discussed, and eventually she'll get there.'

'She…? What are you talking about? Who?' His words floated into the empty space in front of him. Sebastián had already walked away.

What the hell was wrong with this hospital? It had been three days since he'd started here, and he already had a notebook full of suggestions of things that needed to change in both the trauma department and the ER for them to be more efficient. One of these changes, Carlos guessed, wouldn't make him the most popular surgeon in the department. Not that he cared much. His placement at different hospitals was fleeting for various reasons. Sticking around for too long meant getting attached to people. His days of being attached to anyone had ended five years ago—when his wife died in a car accident.

That night was the reason he was here, the reason he'd never settled down in one place for longer than a few months.

'Did you hear about Dr Martinez? Apparently, the…' Carlos caught the snippet of discussion as two doctors walked past him, heads turned to each other. His gaze followed them, and he had no doubt they were gossiping about what had happened between them in the OR. Throughout the day, he had heard different retellings of the story—and the embellishments as it had passed from one staff member to the other were concerning.

How could they take their work seriously when they were so busy talking about their colleagues? People's personal lives had no place in the hospital. He would never dream of bringing up Rosa…

Carlos pushed the thought of his wife away and straightened his spine. His primary concern right now was Sofia Martinez. Because clearly she was letting some personal issue impede their working relationship. He couldn't have one surgeon avoiding him, potentially causing more distracting rumours to fly around the hospital. No, he'd correct whatever misconception she had about him right now.

He took a deep breath as his hand landed on the door handle, a flutter in his chest giving him pause. In the last three hospitals he'd been at, he had always met people who were unhappy about the changes he'd recommended. Even though Sofia was behaving this way, she didn't strike him as someone to reject an opportunity to learn. When they had performed their surgery together, he'd even sensed something akin to closeness, recognising how their styles in surgery complimented each other.

Before he could overanalyse their compatibility in the OR, Carlos pushed the door open and slipped in through a slim crack before closing it again—coming face-to-face with Sofia Martinez, who stood only two handbreadths away from him.

The awareness of her proximity to him flared into life in the pit of his stomach, shooting hot tendrils of fire across his body. Overwhelmed by the sensation, he took a step back and started when his back collided with the door he'd just come through.

Carlos stood so close he could count the golden flecks in her brown eyes. They formed tiny constellations he was sure he would love to memorise if he just got enough chances to look at her uninterrupted.

The thoughts kept bubbling up inside of him unbidden and resisting his efforts to pull himself back into the moment. Seconds ticked on in which they were just staring at each other, waiting for the other one to break the stare.

'Did you need something, Dr Cabrera? Maybe some directions?' Sofia finally asked, pulling him out of his stupor. Ice coated her words, but he could have sworn that there was a slight tremble in her voice.

The speech he had prepared before opening the door was gone. So were any clever retorts he might have had. Hell, he could barely remember what had possessed him to come in here. Maybe he did really need some directions…

'Why are you running away from me?' He shot the question at her with no additional filtering, his mind too preoccupied with her sudden proximity to care about delicacy.

The sooner they sorted this out, the faster he could leave.

Sofia's eyes rounded, and he glimpsed a sliver of white around the dark brown. She blinked several times, her long lashes sweeping over her cheeks with each bat and drawing all of his attention towards them. That was until her lower lip vanished between her teeth for a fraction of a second, but long enough for Carlos to notice.

'I'm not running away from you,' she said, and at least she had the decency to blush at the obvious lie they both knew she had just uttered. A blush that tinted her cheeks in a warm, sun-kissed apricot.

His fingers contracted into a fist at his side as the urge to brush over her skin tingled in his fingertips. What was wrong with him?

'If you're not avoiding me, what's the reason

you're in here?' he asked after clearing his throat to get rid of any residual huskiness.

'I...' Her quick glance up and down the shelves revealed her intention as she started speaking. Her hand shot up, looking to grab anything that she could plausibly need in this moment, and Carlos almost felt bad for her when she dropped it with a sigh.

'Fine... Even if I was hiding in here from you, what's it to you? You're not *interested* in hearing my excuses, are you?' she said, and squared her shoulders as she looked back at him.

It was Carlos's turn to blink. Had he been too abrasive with her? He knew people perceived him as direct, but that was one quality that had earned him the success in his field he enjoyed now. There was no room for waiting or hesitation in trauma surgery. He strived to embody those principles—and he expected the staff he worked with to do the same.

But he was here to teach, and he could see now that he'd fallen short of that. Otherwise, Sofia would know why he'd said what he had.

'The patient's airway became blocked during transport. You had to stop to perform an emergency tracheotomy,' he said.

In the silence between them, he could hear the sharp intake of breath at his words. Had she thought him unkind for no good reason other than being in a hurry to get the patient ready for surgery?

'That's right,' she said, pushing out her chin in a silent challenge that Carlos wanted to meet—and forced himself not to. This wasn't the first time an antagonistic employee who viewed him as an intruder had confronted him. Meeting them with the same intensity had never ended well.

Something about Sofia made him want to throw things back at her because he knew she could take it, and he wanted to see how far they could push each other. Strictly professionally, of course.

'And you think that when our patient is flatlining and about to bleed out, it's the right time to listen to the reasons you were late?' Despite trying his best, he couldn't keep the edge out of his words completely. It was a sharpness he had honed over the last five years, a weapon he wielded so no one would ever dare to get too close to him. If they all perceived him as an unpleasant and elitist surgeon, it would be easier to leave at the end of the assignment—because when Rosa had died all these years ago, his capability of forming connections to people on any emotional level went with her.

Sofia stared at him, her big eyes unblinking, and he could almost see the wheels turning inside her head.

'There is a time and place for explanations,' he said when she remained quiet, only the clenching muscle in her jaw showing any kind of outward reaction. 'When a patient lands in our OR, the only things we should be interested in are the facts that will help us perform the surgery better. We can discuss anything else in the patient notes.'

The woman still stared at him, though her eyes had narrowed further, and he would have laughed at her unwillingness to give him even a little bit of acknowledgement. Stubbornness was a trait he knew all too well. It was another reason he had made it so far as a surgeon.

'Explanations, yes, I agree,' Sofia finally said, her voice a low rumble that vibrated through the air between them. Had her voice been this deep a few moments ago? Or were his ears playing tricks on him?

Carlos didn't get the chance to contemplate it further as she continued, 'But you specifically said excuses. I never intended to give you any excuses because I don't need to justify my lateness when it hinges on getting the patient to you alive. I'm all for you being here and helping the trauma team reach the next level. But remember that the words you use do matter, Dr Cabrera.'

'Carlos.' His name flew out of his mouth before he could reconsider it, the offer to call him by his first name floating between them like an untethered ghost.

Why had he just volunteered that? He didn't want to be close to Sofia or anyone else at this place. No, the same rules applied as always. Carlos would do his best to equip the staff with all of his teachings and processes before moving on to the next place.

Yet here he was, offering his first name to this strangely disarming woman standing in front of him with crossed arms and a defiant sparkle in her golden-brown eyes.

'Carlos,' she echoed when the silence between them extended, as if she needed to try it on for size, and his name from her lips shot a flash of heat through his body that settled in the pit of his stomach with an uncomfortable pinch.

His breath was audible in the confines of the small supply closet, and he regretted following her into this tiny space to begin with. She was too close to him, noticed each reaction as her intelligent eyes raked over him, and now he could no longer control the steadiness of his breathing.

'I agree that the words I use do matter, and I will take that feedback on board. I might have come here to teach you all, but that doesn't mean I'm above learning new things myself. I appreciate your openness,' he said, in part because he genuinely meant it, but also to end this conversation and finally get back into the ER where the air wasn't as hot and filled with electric sparks that were threatening to burst into flames all over his skin. 'Rules and norms are important to me. If you feel like I'm not embodying them, I would like to know.'

Carlos braced himself for another barbed retort, but her lips parted in a genuine smile. He didn't know how to react as more heat surged through his veins, forcing him to expel another ragged breath.

'That might be the first thing we have in common. Sebastián has, on more than one occasion, described me as "aggressively by the book". He makes it sound like I need to loosen up, but I don't see any reasons to change,' she said, the smile tugging on her lips reaching her eyes and giving them a soft sparkle.

'You won't catch me trying to change that about you. If anything, that's something I encourage in the staff I teach. We need to think on our feet and have enough agency to go with whatever is needed in the moment. But to do that, we need to know all of our internal processes inside and out, and adhere to certain standards.' Speaking about that set his frayed nerves at ease, letting him sink into a topic he had a full mastery of and knew how to navigate.

'So, what made you fall in love with rules and regulations?' she asked as she leaned against the wall in a gesture far too casual for his liking.

'Excuse me?' Half of his effort went into remembering that they were still in a professional setting, with the faint buzzing and humming from the ER filtering through the door. Carlos couldn't remember a single instance in his career when he had spent a prolonged time in a supply closet. The poor ventilation in here was evident from the flush creeping up his neck. The lack of oxygen was clearly heating him up.

'I've found that with people like us, there is one defining event in their lives that…well, that made us who we are,' she continued, and he scanned her face for the same flush rising in him. All he found was perfect caramel skin. 'Mine was in elementary school. We only had one ball to play with, so every day, a different group got to play with it. Some kids banded together to rig the system. Massive nerd that I am, I came up with a fair schedule for the ball. My teacher was very impressed with the effort. Implementing that timetable is still one of my career highlights.'

The tension rippling through his body ebbed as he considered her words, and he raised one eyebrow. 'Did you just make a joke?'

Sofia frowned. 'Joke? I'm dead serious. To this

day, the school still uses the schedule for play-time.'

'I see…' The chuckle bubbled up in Carlos's chest without him being able to stop it, and grew louder when Sofia joined in. 'Rules have led to tremendous successes in your life. I can see why they are important to you.'

That was about as much he wanted to know about Sofia Martinez. While he understood the argument that getting to know a person well improved collaboration, he wouldn't be a long-term addition to the team. Familiarity would only chain him down.

Judging by how her gaze narrowed on him, Carlos got the sense that she had picked up on his deflection tactic. 'What about you? What event made Carlos Cabrera fall in love with rules?'

Carlos didn't know what compelled him to answer truthfully when he had been so close to escaping. Something about Sofia, a quality she possessed, was strangely disarming. Maybe be-cause they had found the one thing they could agree on in an otherwise contentious relationship?

'I lost someone important to me,' he said, and the regret rushing into his system was instanta-neous and gut-wrenching.

Her features softened, and the familiar gleam of sympathy entered her eyes. An understandable reaction, but one Carlos hated seeing. He didn't deserve anyone's pity, not when he had been the one driving the car on the night of the accident that had killed his wife.

'Oh, I'm sorry…' Sofia breathed out, her voice trailing off when he shook his head.

Before he could say anything else he might regret, Carlos reached behind him, grasping the door handle while still facing her. 'Glad we cleared this up, Martinez,' he said, then turned to leave. Her sharp intake of breath stopped him.

Her eyes were wide when he shot her a glance over his shoulder, and he didn't miss how they darted down his body, as if taking in his entire frame. Her lips parted, and there was another rushed exhale he couldn't quite place. 'If I'm to call you Carlos, it's only right if you call me Sofia.'

Something about her tone told him that this concession cost her as much as his had him— though the reasons for it were much different. He wanted to ask what they were, but quickly squashed that impulse. Knowing what made her tick wasn't essential for him to do his job, and he already knew way too much about her.

'All right… Sofia,' he said, and caught himself savouring her name on his tongue. The awareness of his attraction to her, of her closeness to him, lanced through him and morphed into a flash of panic that had him throwing the door open and leaving the supply closet—before he could do anything he would regret.

CHAPTER THREE

THE ENCOUNTER WITH Carlos in the supply closet lingered in Sofia's mind—no matter how hard she tried to forget. One of the main reasons for her repeated failures was the man himself. There wasn't a single day when she wouldn't see him, and the flashes of heat that caused erupted through her without her bidding.

Sofia shook her head, angry at herself and reminding herself that she should be irritated with Carlos as well. The reason she was seeing him everywhere she went had to do with the fact that this man didn't understand boundaries.

'We can give these antibiotics alongside his regular insulin shots?' The familiar voice of Mariana Flores, the charge nurse of the emergency room, pierced through the heavy fog of her thoughts, and Sofia blinked once.

'Sorry what?' She looked down and read the text on the tablet Mariana held towards her, scanning the medication order for her post-op patient. 'This is fine. There shouldn't be any interference.'

The nurse flashed her a smile. 'Where did your mind wander off to?'

'Nowhere good,' she mumbled as a reply, then hesitated before tapping on the tablet and bringing up the OR schedule of the trauma department. She told herself that she wasn't checking what surgery was happening in OR Two and that she needed to know occupancy in case an emergency came in.

But she wasn't fooling herself, or the woman standing on the other side of the counter. 'Checking in on Cabrera? I didn't take you for someone who fancies him,' she said with a chuckle that sent a flush crawling up Sofia's neck.

'I don't fancy him. Quite the opposite. I'm checking on him so I can avoid him. This guy has absolutely no respect for how we run our trauma rooms here. Every time I turn around, he's already in the ambulance bay, stealing yet another one of my patients. He's such a pain to work with.'

Carlos had been here one week already, and rather than teaching her the things she needed to learn, he was turning her routine upside down with his constant interference. Sometimes he even had the audacity to suggest that she assist on a surgery she had every right to be the leading surgeon on. Those were the actions of a man who was completely full of himself.

'That's not what I hear from everyone else,' Mariana said, a grin on her lips. 'Yesterday someone brought him a casserole after he mentioned he doesn't have enough time to cook.'

'I know, and don't you think that's super-weird? Especially since he gives away half of the gifts he receives. He got a plate of *alfajores*, and he looked me dead in the eye as he tried to palm them off on me.'

She had pinned him with a withering look, unsure if he was genuinely interested in giving her cookies or if this was some weird mind-game he was playing with her. Someone who so blatantly stole her surgeries wouldn't shy away from other methods of throwing her off.

'But you like *alfajores*.'

'That's not the point, Mariana. Stealing people's surgeries and passing along gifts he was given is rude. Why won't anyone acknowledge that?' She curled her hand into a fist, tapping it against the counter separating her from the nurse.

Mariana lifted her hands in front of her. 'Hey, don't drag me into this mess of unresolved feelings you have for Cabrera.'

Sofia snorted at that, hoping she'd put enough derision into the sound to get her point across. Her heart had jumped into her mouth at Mariana's words, recalling the moment they had shared in the supply closet. His proximity had flooded her with awareness, the scent of spicy pine still lingering around her whenever she closed her eyes. The tension between them had reached a new level.

But then he had opened up and let her glimpse beyond the mask he wore at work every day. Something had unravelled from him, a thin, gossamer thread that connected them—because they had found common ground.

Had she imagined the electricity crackling between them? She didn't usually daydream about colleagues. Her job was way too important to her for some fanciful crushes on *gringo* doctors who came to work at the Hospital General. Especially after the last man she'd opened up to had repaid her trust by betraying her so deeply, she still kept a close guard on her feelings.

Yet somehow Carlos kept sneaking back into her thoughts. Ugh, Sofia needed to get him out of her head. How had he even become so stuck in there in the first place?

'Let me go to the ER before he can magically appear there and mess with my head some more,' she muttered, more to herself than to Mariana. Then she turned away from the nurse and trotted back to the ER. She could catch up with her patient charts while she waited for the next emergency to come through the doors—and hopefully beat Carlos to it.

As she pushed the doors to the emergency room open, she ran into a tall wall of lean muscle. The scent of woodsy spice filled her nose, a delicious—and familiar—aroma. Her head whipped upwards as she collided with Carlos Cabrera.

'How on earth are you already down here? Is it your mission to make me go nuts? Is that why we hired you?' He was supposed to be in surgery. She had just checked that two minutes ago.

He tilted his head to the side, and the inquisitive look on his face was so flattering to his features that Sofia wanted to both shove him and kiss him just to wipe that expression away. The second thought was one that concerned her. Why was she even thinking about Carlos in such a context when she had nothing but contempt for him? One tiny slice of vulnerability shared in a supply closet couldn't be enough to change her mind about him.

'What are you talking about?' he asked, and Sofia had to take several breaths to banish the fantasy of their lips connecting. Where had that come from?

'I was upstairs and saw your name on the board. But since you are standing here, right when I'm trying to get back to work, I have to assume you are some kind of *demonio* sent to torment me.'

'A demon? Really, Sofia?' The smirk pulling

at the corners of his lips transformed his already handsome face into something from another planet. Her name from his lips sent a bolt of lightning down her spine.

Her mouth went dry as she tried her best to stay present in this conversation. It was probably all part of the *demonio*'s plan—setting her off-kilter. Though she still didn't know why he was going to so much trouble when he wasn't going to stick around. Who was he trying so hard for that he would steal her patients right from under her nose?

'I can't explain it in any other way,' she said after a few beats of silence.

'And what exactly is *it*?' His voice was almost a drawl, hitting her low in the stomach, where the electricity of his scent was already pooling and making it hard to form any cohesive thoughts.

What was wrong with her? Sure, it had been a while since she'd broken things off with Daniel, but was she really so starved for physical closeness that the first handsome doctor to stumble into her path had her brain all scrambled? Was that what was happening here?

'You've been stealing *my* patients and doing *my* surgeries. Even when I'm supposed to be by myself. I thought you came here to train us,' she said, crossing her arms in front of her to give her hands something to hold on to. Because her fingertips were tingling with the strange need to reach out and feel that smirk under her fingers. 'You should be in OR Two, taking care of the trauma case that came in an hour ago.'

His smile dimmed at that. The contrast between his smirking expression and this stern one was so stark that regret flooded her veins, even though she didn't know why he'd stopped smiling—or if it was because of her.

'The patient didn't make it. By the time we got to the operating room, he had already flatlined,' he said, with the cool detachment of someone who had delivered such a message countless times—both to colleagues and the affected family members.

'Oh…' she breathed out, suddenly feeling foolish for her rant and calling him a demon.

Sofia didn't know how she would have reacted were she on the receiving end of her speech, but the contemplative look on his face wasn't what she had expected—and the shiver running down her spine as his dark eyes raked over her was an unpleasant side effect of their whole interaction. Why was he looking at her like that?

And what was going on with her that she even cared? She was no better than any of the other staff members fawning over Carlos whenever they saw him. Something about him was impossible to resist, a form of silent charm that he deployed at will to enchant the people around him.

They remained locked in silence, and just like in the supply closet, the air between them filled with an electric current connecting their bodies. That was until he said, 'As for the stealing of patients and surgeries, I'm simply admitting the patients that come in through the ER. If you feel you are missing out on surgeries, I suggest you get to the patients before I do.'

The tension between them collapsed. Sofia's eyes widened at his words and at the nonchalance in his voice. 'Are you implying I'm not present enough in the emergency room when cases come in?' she said, keeping her voice as calm and quiet as she could.

This guy knew exactly how to get under her skin, and by the grin spreading over his lips, she could guess that he got great satisfaction out of that. 'I'm not implying anything. Surgery is competitive, and I can't wait around for you to take the patients on when they're coming into the ER. You know our certification as a trauma centre is at risk if the wait times for surgeries get too high. I can't let that happen on my watch,' he said, as if she was a year one intern who had just begun her first day in the emergency room.

'Oh, no, Carlos. You're not putting this on me. You're the one who seems to live at the hospital.

How else are you *always* here, even when I'm scheduled as the trauma surgeon on call for a shift? With how much time you spend here, I feel sorry for whoever waits for you to come home. Are you married?' The last question came out before she could consider whether she *really* wanted to know. Except she wanted to know. The sheer chemistry brewing between them demanded an answer—though she didn't plan on doing anything with that information. Even if he was single, she wasn't interested in any kind of relationship. Not when she was still picking up the pieces of herself from the last one.

A shadow fluttered over his expression, a spark of hurt entering his eyes for but a second before it disappeared along with the smirk—leaving nothing but a stony expression behind. The shake of his head was a short one as he said, 'No, I'm not.'

Sofia sensed there was more to the story than that short answer let on, and she clamped down on the urge to pry for more information. The sentence *So you're available for some fun?* formed in her head without her bidding, and those words cascaded through her in hot and cold waves. Was that what was happening to her? Did she yearn for some closeness with a man with no strings or promises attached to it? It had been a while since she'd just enjoyed herself without any worries, and even though she hated to admit it, Carlos was definitely her type. With his cut jawline and high cheekbones, Sofia believed he would be many people's type, and he could have anyone he wanted.

Except when she'd asked him about being married, he'd looked almost pained for a split second. Was the person he lost maybe his wife? Sofia wasn't sure it was any of her business to even ask.

'Ambulance inbound. Still awaiting details from the paramedics on the patient. Trauma surgery support requested at the ambulance bay.' The announcement snapped both of them out of their thoughts, their heads whirling around to the door leading to the ambulances. Then Carlos looked over at her, the smirk she had seen before back on his lips.

'I had a good time doing surgery with you the other day, so let's work on this one together,' he said before rushing off, forcing Sofia to follow.

That announcement had come just at the right time. Carlos hurried down the corridor leading to the access way, where the ambulance services came in with patients. Rushing down here gave him enough time to put his head on straight again after Sofia had knocked him sideways more than once during their exchange—along with the unbidden heat that her proximity sparked.

Are you married?

It was because of questions like that one that he never stayed in one place long enough to get to know anyone. How could he possibly admit to his marriage when he had failed the one person he'd promised to protect for the rest of his life?

He couldn't escape his guilt over the car accident, and the part he'd played in it, so he remained untethered from any form of emotional closeness. Carlos was content in his solitude, regretting forever how his marriage had ended too soon.

Those were the things he reminded himself of as he approached the doors to the ambulance bay with Sofia on his heels.

The effect she had on him was concerning, and the fierceness of the attraction snapping into place between them shook him to his core. How could he feel attracted to the one person in the hospital who was openly hostile towards him? There was no way the feeling wasn't one-sided, which brought the entire thing to a new level of inappropriate. Not only were they colleagues, but he was also leaving before they would even have the chance to explore anything.

Not that he had anything to explore. Carlos was here to work and nothing else. Affairs and no-strings-attached arrangements were for people whose hearts weren't as broken as his. Though neither of those things involved emotional attachment, they still required a clear head and conscience. He didn't have either. So whatever tendrils of attraction were floating around between them were best forgotten. He knew that would be the best for everyone involved. Yet his heart still slammed against his chest as if it was trying to escape when Sofia stepped up next to him.

Her scent was intoxicating, and it wasn't for the first time this week that he wondered if she wore perfume or if she would still smell like that as he peeled each layer of clothing off her body.

'Any more details about the incoming case?' Sofia asked as an intern stepped through the doors.

'This is an overflow coming in from Centro Médico Evita Perón. They don't have any more trauma bays open after an MVA involving several vehicles,' the intern said, reading the notes off her phone.

A cold shower trickled down Carlos's spine, a reaction familiar to him, yet he still hated it. He forced a deep breath down his nose, clamping down on the trauma reaction bubbling up in his veins. The intern had said there was a car crash, not that their case was part of one. They might have moved an unrelated case here because there was no space left in the trauma bays at the other hospital because of the MVA.

Though it had been five years since he'd been

in his accident, there were still moments that brought back the memories in a vivid flash. Another reason for him to never open up to anyone around him. How could he be a trauma surgeon when he struggled to operate on car crash victims? Both medication and therapy had helped him cope, but grounding techniques could only get him so far in the chaotic environment of the OR.

'Carlos.' Hearing his name snapped him out of his dark thoughts, and he turned his head. Sofia gave him a sidelong glance with a fine line between her brows. There was a touch of softness he hadn't seen in her before as she asked, 'You okay?'

Damn, had he been that obvious about the turmoil going on inside of him? He forced his usual mask of aloofness back onto his face, staring ahead as the ambulance approached with its sirens echoing off the walls. The part of him that wanted to remain distant from everyone at the hospital wanted to ignore the question, but there was another part that appreciated the attention, even if he didn't deserve it.

'I'm…' He hesitated, searching for the right words to say. Foreboding mounted in him as he watched the vehicle approach, but he couldn't say anything. 'I didn't sleep well,' he said, settling on a plausible lie for whatever Sofia had seen in him. Then he stepped forward as the ambulance came to a halt in front of them.

The doors burst open as the paramedic stepped out of the back, dragging a stretcher with the unconscious patient. His other hand was holding an Ambu bag and squeezing it in calm intervals. As he approached, the intern stepped forward and took over delivering oxygen to the unconscious patient.

'What do you have for us, Gabriel?' Sofia asked as she grabbed the handles of the stretcher.

'We have a female patient in her thirties, involved in a high-speed MVA. She suffered significant trauma to the chest with decreased breath sounds on the left side. Potential pneumothorax,' the paramedic rattled off, keeping pace with Carlos and Sofia as they pushed the stretcher up the corridor. 'We've had to put her on supplemental oxygen and administered fluids and painkillers as per protocol.'

The edges of his vision darkened as he looked down at the patient, feeling the weight of old memories crashing down on him and constricting his chest. Breathing became harder with each step, and Carlos fought to keep the rising panic at bay. This was *not* her, and unlike with Rosa, he had a chance to help this woman come away with her life intact.

He caught another glance from Sofia, and her

expression conveyed the same question she'd asked him just a few moments ago. But then her focus shifted onto the paramedic. 'What's her blood pressure?'

'Last measure was one-ten over seventy, with an elevated heart rate and a pulse ox of ninety percent,' Gabriel replied, his eyes darting between Sofia and Carlos as he gave the update.

'Lower oxygen saturation could mean you're right about the punctured lung. We should get an emergency X-ray to figure out our next steps.' Sofia looked at him. Not for confirmation. He knew that well enough after the conversation they'd had earlier today.

No, for some reason, she was checking in with him, as if she could sense the overwhelming sensations creeping in on him. Could she? His reputation as a knowledgeable surgeon who could work under pressure was the reason he could get a job wherever he wanted. Part of it was keeping a tight grip on any PTSD symptoms. So far, not a single person he'd worked with had mentioned anything.

Yet Sofia was looking at him as if she could read every single thought and see the tension in him.

So he nodded in response, and they continued to push the gurney forward. Carlos stepped up to the sink as they entered the trauma room with the patient, cleaning his sweat-slick palms before pulling on the gloves. 'I'll get the portable X-ray ready,' he said as he turned around, avoiding looking too closely at the patient. He only needed a minute to step away and collect himself.

'Set up the supplementary oxygen so she's ready for the X-ray,' Sofia said, then rattled off more instructions to the people in the trauma bay.

The confrontation with her earlier had triggered long-dormant tendrils of attraction that he didn't want to feel or even consider. Mixing that with the trauma trigger of the accident had created an explosive cocktail of stress-induced reactions inside of him. This was the worst possible moment for any of this.

'We're good to go on the X-rays,' he said, clenching his jaw when his voice came out brittle. His mind raced, wondering if he should extract himself from this situation. Sofia had it in hand, and even though they had their disagreements on methods, he trusted in her excellence as a doctor.

'Oxygen is flowing. Everyone step outside for the X-ray.' Sofia waved at the intern assisting them. They all walked out of the room to avoid unnecessary exposure to radiation. After they heard the whirring of the machine followed by a buzz, they all streamed back into the room. The images would only take a few seconds to appear on the screens, but there wasn't a second to lose in stabilising the patient while they waited.

Sofia and the intern approached the patient, both looking at him for instructions. They were expecting him to run this trauma room. Carlos took a deep breath while trying his hardest to keep his mind on assessing the situation as a doctor. But when he saw the blood of an open cut clinging to the dark brown skin, the black hair half-down from the bun it had been in—a hairstyle he used to see every morning after waking up—his breath faltered.

'Her pulse is rising. She's in distress,' the intern said as she took her stethoscope out and placed it on the patient's chest. 'Reduced breath sounds on the right side.'

'Carlos?' Sofia said his name, a soft sound laced with concern, but he could hardly hear it over the rush of his own blood through his ears. Darkness crept in on him, blurring his vision, and each breath was harder than the next. The beeping of the monitor drilled into his ears, the fluorescent light suddenly glaring, forcing him to avert his eyes.

In this state, he couldn't work on any patients. He needed to get out of here.

'I'm…needed elsewhere. Run the trauma room, Martinez. I'll send someone to assist,' he said, hoping his voice didn't sound as choked as he felt. Then he turned around without another word as more visions of the past threatened to overwhelm him.

'Good job, everyone,' Sofia said as they wheeled the patient out of the trauma room and to the intensive care unit.

The car crash had broken several of her ribs. One of them had punctured her left lung, just as the delivering paramedic, Gabriel, had suspected. The pneumothorax was small, thankfully, and could be treated with the right pain management and bed rest. After stabilising the patient's breathing, they had stitched up the cuts and checked for other injuries. As far as car crash victims were concerned, she was one of the luckier ones, having escaped any devastating injuries.

Now that she was done with the patient, she could turn her mind to the thing that she'd stowed away in a separate compartment of her brain so she could put all of her attention on her work. She quickly went by the nurses' station to see if there were any more incoming cases and was glad when the nurse shook her head. She had some time to spare just when she needed it—or rather, when Carlos needed it.

Considering the calm and experience he'd brought into every single surgery they'd worked on together, his behaviour in the trauma room was highly unusual. He'd completely frozen when he'd seen the patient. Was she someone he knew? Panic had radiated out from him, enough for Sofia to pick up on it, and just as she had been about to ask him what was wrong, he had excused himself.

Sofia walked up and down the different beds and treatment rooms to see if he had simply stepped away to look after another incoming case. But he wasn't there, and when she called the charge nurse to ask if he was in surgery, the woman said she hadn't seen him since he went down to the emergency room. So he was still here somewhere…

She paused when her eyes fell onto the closed door of the supply closet where they'd had their rather intense exchange last week. The hair along her arms rose as she stared at the door, a strange sensation coming over her. Would he have sought refuge in the space they had shared? Or was she spinning up some strange connection to him to justify the intensity of her own reaction to him?

It wouldn't hurt to check either way. Worst-case scenario, she was making things up in her head. But if he was there and in need of help… The look on his face had been unlike any she'd ever seen on him. No swagger, none of the bravado of a surgeon who knew he was the top-ranking one in his field. Just something pure and naked, something he usually allowed no one to see.

Shaking off the memory, she stepped to the door and pushed the handle down, sticking her head through the crack. Carlos stood behind the door, his back facing her, and she could tell he was breathing in quick bursts by the way his shoulders rose and fell. She stepped into the closet, closing the door behind her and twisting the lock.

The lights were off, the only source of light whatever crept through the gaps around the edges of the door. Sofia scanned the shelves stuffed with medical equipment needed to run an efficient ER, giving her eyes time to adjust to the dimness.

'Carlos, it's me,' she said when he didn't react to her intrusion, stepping closer to his side.

She frowned as she looked at him. Even with limited light, she could see that the colour had drained from his face, leaving a dull, pale imitation of his warm-toned skin. His eyes were staring ahead almost sightlessly. Slipping her hand around his arm, she pressed her index and middle fingers onto the inside of his wrist, counting the beats of his heart. Her frown deepened, and her hand lingered on his arm, his skin cold to her touch.

'I think you're having a panic attack,' she said

softly, her hand tightening on his arm in an effort to get him to acknowledge her.

Panic attacks were far too common among trauma surgeons. With the pressure they were under to assess patients efficiently and accurately, as a professional group, they rarely took enough time to look after themselves. How could they make that a priority when their days were often twelve hours long, depending on what surgeries they were pulled into? Many colleagues developed PTSD due to witnessing severe injuries and low survival rates, even in top trauma departments.

'We need to slow down your breathing. The hyperventilation is only worsening the other symptoms.' A chill ran down her spine when Carlos turned his face to finally look at her, his expression stricken. Acting on instinct alone, she reached for his other hand and lifted them both up to place them on her chest.

'You know how to do deep breathing. I watched you do it earlier when you sensed the panic attack coming,' she said. Then she took a deep breath of her own and guided him to follow her example.

Carlos did, taking stuttering breaths in and out. He slowed down somewhat, but not enough to take him out of the state of panic and ground him. Sofia rifled through her brain, thinking of other grounding techniques she'd learned during her training. With the amount of experience Carlos had as a medical professional, he probably had his own set of exercises he liked to go through.

'How can I help you? Would it help to talk me through your triggers, or do you prefer to be grounded with distraction?' Sofia clamped down on her own panic as she asked those questions. Considering how private Carlos had been from the moment he had arrived at the hospital a week ago, he probably didn't want her witnessing his vulnerable moment. They were already on shaky ground with each other, and this interaction wouldn't improve that.

But he needed help, and as much as they grated on each other, Sofia couldn't just walk away and leave him alone.

She breathed out a sigh when his fingers tightened around hers, and his eyes came into focus. The intensity of his stare took her by surprise, cascading a heat down her spine that was becoming way too familiar.

'Pressure,' Carlos said, his voice low and thick, the struggle to verbalise this one word evident.

Sofia opened her mouth to ask what he meant by that, when the pieces clicked into place. His technique to combat rising panic was deep pressure. She glanced around, her eyes running over the shelves in search of something that would help her apply some full-body pressure to him. The hospital had weighted blankets for that purpose, but they weren't in the emergency room.

No, she would have to do it herself. 'Okay,' she said with a nod, more for herself than him, and let go of his hands. 'I can do that.'

She swallowed the sudden lump in her throat at the thought of being so close to Carlos when she had struggled to keep her composure around him ever since their last encounter in this closet. This wasn't about her or the flashes of attraction she was trying so hard to combat. If this was any other colleague, she wouldn't hesitate to wrap them into a hug if it would help.

Carlos was just another colleague. That's what Sofia told herself as she stepped closer to him and wrapped her arms around his torso, squeezing as she held him close to her.

Tiny fires erupted underneath her skin all across her body, but she ignored them along with the swooping sensation that his broad chest pressed against hers caused in her stomach. His arms remained at his sides, his muscles rigid, but as she kept her grip on him tight, his breathing gradually eased into a slower rhythm, his chest rising and falling in a more measured way.

Her warmth seemed to seep into him, his skin becoming warmer where she was in contact with it. 'Try to relax one more muscle with each breath,' she said next to his ear, and couldn't help but sigh when she felt him follow her instructions.

His legs relaxed first, bringing his entire body closer to her as the tension left him. His arms and torso followed, becoming soft under her, and then finally his head slumped forwards, coming to rest on her shoulder with a drawn-out exhale.

Sofia kept her hold on him and continued to take deep breaths of her own, setting a pace Carlos could follow. He did, his breath soon syncing with hers as they stood in the dimly lit supply closet, absorbing the quiet energy around them.

She didn't know how long they stood there with her holding him close to her or at what point she'd got lost in this simple touch. A rush of awareness flooded through her when Carlos's hands came to rest on her waist, drawing her closer into his front. His head still rested on her shoulder, his nose nuzzling into a sensitive spot on her neck. He breathed deeply and steadily now, each exhale sending a skitter of electricity down her spine as it blew against her skin.

His hands wandered up her back, his face moving closer, and she leaned into his touch as warmth pooled in her stomach and shot spears of delicious heat through her body.

'*Gracias,*' he whispered, and his lips grazed the shell of her ear in a whisper of a touch.

Sofia's breath caught in her throat, and an involuntary moan escaped her lips. The sound was loud in the confines of the supply closet. It ripped through the air that had, until this moment, only been filled with their quiet breaths.

Carlos lifted his head, and she took a sharp inhale when their gazes collided. His face was close enough to hers that if she stood on her toes, she could slide her mouth right over his. The glint in his eyes was primal and mirrored the erupting sparks of attraction ricocheting inside her.

Were they really going to…?

'Carlos… I didn't mean to…' Sofia forced the words out of her mouth, her throat thick from the tension between them. She wasn't sure she wanted this. But, more importantly, she didn't know if *he* wanted it, or if they were acting on some impulse that sprung out of their forced proximity.

Carlos took a deep breath, his chest trembling underneath her hands. He blinked twice, and each time the passion faded more—until only confusion remained.

The fire shooting higher within her banked when she beheld the shock spreading over his face. A second later, his hands dropped from her body, and he took a step back, almost colliding with a shelf.

Tension snapped into place between them, accentuated by the silence that spread. Sofia struggled to find the right words to say. The situation had morphed from one thing to the other without her understanding when it had happened—and by the look on Carlos's face, neither had he.

She opened her mouth, needing to say something to cut the tension, but then snapped it shut again when Carlos shook his head.

'You…' he started, but then paused and tilted his head upwards, exposing the column of his throat to her. Sofia stared at it, the urge to lean forward and taste it thundering through her.

As if he had sensed her stare, his eyes came back down to hers. He ran his hand through his short hair, expelling a heavy sigh. 'I'm not… This isn't what… Damn.'

Carlos swore as he shook his head again. Then he turned the lock, ripping the door open and leaving in a hurried step before Sofia had the chance to process what he'd tried to say, and leaving her to puzzle over what had just happened on her own.

CHAPTER FOUR

THE WEEK WENT by without Sofia seeing much of Carlos. After their second encounter in the supply closet, it seemed as if he was now avoiding her. She would have laughed at how they had switched places if she wasn't overwhelmed and confused about what had happened—or why he was avoiding her.

Was he ashamed that he'd had a panic attack? She didn't think his confidence was so fragile. Especially since he was a physician who had admitted on his first day to the assembled staff how hard the trauma department could be on one's psyche. He'd cited this as one reason the hospital's leadership had hired him to work here. More efficient workflows would mean less stress and more freedom to focus on the things that truly mattered.

'Did you see how Adriana got rejected by that new surgeon guy? She had…' The fragment of conversation drifted towards her, and Sofia forced her feet to keep moving, her eyes trained to the front as she walked towards the doors of the hospital at the end of her shift.

'That new surgeon guy' could only be one person—the same one that had been haunting her thoughts ever since their…thing in the supply closet.

In her head, Sofia was calling it an almost-kiss, though she wasn't sure she should say that out loud, even to Carlos. But she'd had a strong desire to close the gap between them by leaning in. Had wanted it *badly*. It had been easy to ignore her body's reaction to his when his abrasiveness kept her at arm's length.

Until the moment in the supply closet when she had glimpsed what Carlos kept under tight wraps. What she had witnessed had been a rare moment of vulnerability for him, and going by how he'd stormed off afterwards, he hadn't wanted anyone to see him like that. And he had definitely not wanted her to know that the electric current zapping between them wasn't one-sided.

After he had calmed down and grounded himself, his touch had gone from desperate to tender. The ghost of his touch on her back still lingered on her skin every time she closed her eyes, and with it came a rush of desire that sent tiny prickles across her body.

It was because of this reaction that she wanted to talk to Carlos. Sofia could admit that he was unbelievably fine. She wouldn't have been surprised to hear that he had walked off a 'Hot Docs' calendar shoot before coming here. Like all the other women and men in this hospital, she had eyes and could appreciate an attractive man when she saw one.

What had startled her during their encounter had been the heat radiating from *him*. How *he* had touched *her*. Carlos had hovered over her mouth, as if daring her to close the gap between them to claim a kiss she knew in her bones would be mind-blowing. And then the defences had come shooting back up, shaking them both out of their desire-induced stupor, and he had run away— leaving Sofia wondering if what she had sensed building between them was genuine or another of his trauma reactions.

'What's got you so down?' a familiar voice asked as she stepped outside the doors of the hospital on her way home.

Gabriel Romero stood a few paces to the side of the entrance, leaning against the wall of the building. She walked up to him with a smile she hoped didn't look as tired as it felt.

'Hey, Gabe, haven't seen your face since last week.' Gabriel had been the one to deliver the trauma patient from the car crash that had somehow triggered Carlos. Since Sofia spent a lot of her time waiting for ambulances to arrive with patients needing immediate assessment from the trauma team, she'd become familiar with all the paramedics servicing the hospital. She and Gabriel had hit it off well, and they enjoyed a chat whenever they met outside of any emergency situations.

'I keep hoping to see you, *amiga*, but whenever I come in with a case, I see the new guy with a bunch of junior doctors at his side.' Gabriel paused, flashing her a grin before he said, 'He seems to be popular.'

Sofia would have rolled her eyes at that comment two weeks ago, but now heat rushed to her cheeks, and she failed at producing a convincing snort of derision. 'He keeps beating me to any arrivals at the hospital. If I didn't know it better, I would think he's getting some insider information,' she said, deflecting from her own feelings.

Gabriel raised his hands in defence. 'You know I would never double-cross you like that, Fia.'

'Yeah, right,' she grumbled, but the smile she flashed him this time was genuine. 'I know he's doing it to teach the junior staff, but I can't help feeling a bit…set aside.'

His expression sobered as he listened to her, nodding in acknowledgement. 'It's difficult when someone comes into a pre-established dynamic. But he's not being a jerk about it, is he?'

She shook her head. 'No, he's fine. I'm just…'

Sofia paused, unsure if she should talk about what had happened between her and Carlos. But she'd been carrying it around for an entire week with nobody to talk to about it. She'd usually go and talk to Bella, but with her friend's reduced hours now that she was twenty-two weeks pregnant with triplets, she barely got to see the woman any more.

'I don't know what happened when you brought in that patient, but something triggered him that day. He had a panic attack, and I had to talk him down. Since then he's been avoiding me, and I… just don't know what to think of that.' The words were pouring out of her mouth before she could decide whether she should share so much with anyone, but Gabriel was her friend and she could trust him, even if their conversations mostly happened between patients.

'That's a tough spot to be in. We're all exposed to some triggering stuff. Maybe he hasn't had a trigger response in a long time and took it hard?' Gabriel mused, his index finger tapping against his chin.

'Yeah, maybe…' Sofia just thought of that, but if they were correct, then it was even more important for them to talk about it. What if being in a new environment was the triggering part? No one would think any less of him, but they needed to know in case anything happened…

'For what it's worth, I've never seen Cabrera misstep in the cases I brought in, and I'm sure someone of his calibre wouldn't put the hospital at risk like that,' the paramedic said, shrugging his shoulders. 'Though his aloofness is surprising. I would have thought by now *someone* would have cracked his shell open. Newbies rarely stay this closed off with how social the hospital is.'

Sofia huffed at that. 'You're telling me. I just overheard two people talking about him rejecting someone. Maybe because he's leaving at the end of the month, he doesn't think it's worth it...'

'Sounds about right. Even some of the ambulance workers have been trying to get his attention, but he seems very...single-minded.'

Heat prickled in the back of her neck, trickling down over her spine until it pooled in the pit of her stomach. She had experienced his single-mindedness first hand, though being the object of it had been mostly unnerving. *Mostly* because there was a distinct aftertaste of exhilaration flooding through her system every time she thought about their moment.

'Papá!' The shout of a child ripped her out of her thoughts, and as she turned, a young boy hurled himself into Gabriel's arms.

'Hello, *mijo*. You remember Fia?'

Sofia smiled at the boy, raising her hand in a small wave. '*Ola*, Javi. I was wondering why your dad was just standing around here when he could make himself useful.'

The boy laughed at that, just like she had hoped he would. Then Sofia raised her hand at both of them in a small wave. 'I'll get out of your hair. Thanks for listening, Gabe.'

The paramedic nodded with a small smile. 'To be continued.'

Though she had left the hospital almost an hour ago, Sofia wasn't in any hurry to go back home. Her brief conversation with Gabriel had brought up the scene from the other day, and she strolled aimlessly through Buenos Aires as she thought of what to do about the tension between her and Carlos.

As she walked down the winding streets of the inner city, her eyes snagged on something interesting now and then. A cute dress in a store window or some tasty-looking baked goods, making her stop and stare. Nothing was captivating enough to hold her attention for long, her mind drawn back to Carlos and his odd behaviour towards her. That was until she almost walked into a group of young women standing in front of the large window of a store.

Curious what would draw such a crowd, she looked up at the sign above the window. It read

Academia Ritmo de Capoeira. Sofia blinked at the sign and then looked at the assembled women.

Capoeira? She tried forming the word with her mouth, the syllables not quite fitting together and leaving her with a foreign sound in her ear. With the words in front of it saying rhythm academy, it could be some kind of dance? That still didn't explain why such a dance studio would draw the attention of an entire group of women.

Sofia stepped closer, looking in between the heads of the other women, and saw what had grabbed their attention. Through the window, she could see a space that looked more like a gym than a dance studio. Mats covered the entire floor, and a row of shoes was lined up on each side, all different sizes, colours and makes.

A group of people stood in a circle, most of them clapping in a rhythm only they could hear. And in the middle of the circle stood two men facing each other, engaged in something Sofia couldn't put into words. It wasn't quite a dance, at least not one she knew of, but rather an exchange of fluid motions and movements that were some-how connecting the participants, even though nei-ther was touching the other.

The man on the left wore loose-fitting white trousers and a tank top. His hair was more grey than brown, and deep wrinkles surrounded his eyes. Yet despite those indications of age, he moved with a graceful fluidity as he dropped low to evade the incoming leg of the other man— his opponent?

She tracked the leg as the other man dragged it back, her eyes slowly raking further up and taking in that picture of stunning, mouth-watering masculinity. His trousers were the same as the older man's, giving them both an ethereal touch as they moved about the circle. But unlike his opponent, the man on the right had opted to forgo his shirt for the practice, leaving everyone— including herself—to admire the rippling muscles underneath dark brown skin as he flowed back and forth.

Sweat pearled over his skin, and Sofia followed a trail of it over his pecs down his abdomen until the drop disappeared into the trail of hair leading from his navel down to the waistband of his trousers.

'*Ay, Dios mío, qué guapo,*' one of the women in front of her sighed, and Sofia felt herself nod in agreement, her body reacting to sensations that her mind was still catching up to.

He *was* absolutely stunning, and it was no surprise he'd drawn a crowd to watch him dance. Or was it a fight? Sofia still couldn't tell. Whatever it was, the control the man exerted over his body was unearthly, each strike and step a coordination of muscle and strength without sacrificing

grace. Her mouth dried thinking how this fluidity of motion would feel in other circumstances,
some that required even fewer clothes…

If only he would turn his head so she could see
his face. Both men were moving around the circle, but not enough for the younger man to completely face her. Not until a third person entered
the ring of people, gently tapping the man on the
shoulder. Sofia—and the women in front of her—
gasped when he did a cartwheel that ended in a
back-flip that landed close to the circle, his full
front turned towards the window.

Sofia's hand shot up to her mouth in shock as
she looked at his face and recognised who she'd
been thirsting over. Not an anonymous man doing
some sort of fighting dance, but Carlos Cabrera.

He casually looked over the crowd of people
assembled in front of the window, his smile in-
dulgent as the women clapped, and Sofia's heart
stopped in the exact moment their eyes locked.
His smile froze, eyes widening in recognition.
They remained in place like that, neither of them
moving.

A knot tightened in Sofia's stomach, an omen
of the storm that was about to come. She'd already felt increasingly creepy by trying to talk to
him at the hospital. Now he had caught her ogling
him during his time off. Would he even believe

her that she had just come here by chance? Was it too late to pretend she hadn't recognised him?

Her fight-or-flight instincts were warring inside of her, with the latter winning after a short battle—making her turn on her heel and walk down the road.

'I have to go,' Carlos said, following the instinct to go after Sofia as she hurried away.

He gently pushed through the circle and slipped into his sandals while grabbing the loose tank top lying on top of them. Disappointed chatter reached his ears when he stepped outside and pulled his shirt over his head, but he didn't pay it any mind. Sofia was only a few metres ahead of him, and even though he'd been avoiding her the last few days, he didn't stop to think as he went after her.

Coming out of his panic attack with Sofia's arms around him had been like waking up from a nightmare in the middle of the night only to realise that he had never been in any danger because his person was sleeping right next to him, her presence a protective charm.

Only Rosa wasn't here, and it was someone else's touch, someone else's face, that had brought him back to himself. Sofia.

That thought had been haunting him, driving him to avoid her as he tried to sort through the onslaught of emotions rising inside of him. Carlos could no longer deny how attracted he was to her. From the spark in her honey-golden eyes to the messy bun on top of her head, everything about her filled him with a yearning to see this well-composed woman come unravelled under his touch.

'Sofia, wait!' he called after her as she kept on walking. Despite the hesitation that had him avoiding her the last few days, he was unable to stop his pursuit of her. The look on her face had kicked something loose inside of him. An idea that had been growing ever since that moment in the supply closet.

Was his attraction to Sofia the first sign that he was ready for something new? Not a relationship. That would always be out of the question. But maybe some no-strings-attached fun while he was still in town?

Maybe closeness without any commitment was a new way of keeping his struggles inside. The high-pressure situations at work were all about releasing adrenaline to keep him going, but he could get the same effect with endorphins, couldn't he?

Carlos closed the gap between them just as she turned down a side alley. 'Don't you want to talk?' he called after her when she wouldn't stop.

He lengthened his stride, almost colliding

with her when she stopped, turned slowly, and faced him. Her composure was taut, like a tightly wound string ready to snap. '*Now* you want to talk? After I've tried to pin you down for a solid week?'

Her voice shook—though with what emotion he couldn't tell. The volume at which she spoke was as usual, but something elusive weaved itself through her tone.

Despite the flame billowing alive in his chest at her proximity to him, his walls came up around him in an automated defence. 'You never needed some time to process after having a panic attack in front of a colleague?'

Her expression softened at his words, and almost instantly Carlos wished for the quiet tension back. The last thing he needed from her was pity—or her behaviour towards him changing because she thought him fragile. That wasn't what he had come here for.

'You're not the first person to get triggered by something at work. Medical professionals are one of the most likely groups of people to suffer from PTSD symptoms,' she said, and now he wanted the edge in her voice to return. He knew how to deal with someone being annoyed with him. Sympathy tasted like bitter ash in his mouth. They wouldn't be so kind to him if they knew it had been his fault that his wife had died.

The memory of Sofia's body pressed against his in the closet surfaced in his mind as her scent drifted towards him. He held on to that image and let it remind him why he had gone after her. Not to discuss what had already happened, but to see if that mutual attraction could lead to something fun—something distracting. Because the sooner she forgot having seen him so vulnerable, the better. And his instincts were telling him that he had an easy way to replace the image she had of him with a new one. He only had to allow himself to sink deeper into the attraction brewing between them. Use it to keep her thinking about him in a different light.

'I saw you looking at me through the window back there,' he said, deliberately dropping his voice low so it would rumble through the space between them. His tone was suggestive, and he hoped she would be outraged enough to take the bait and forget about the conversation she had started. Whatever it took to get her off the topic of his panic attack—of how she had seen him at his lowest. Maybe that was the best use of the attraction between them. There wasn't a long-term plan here, not with him leaving again so soon. But when she looked at him, Carlos wanted her to see one specific thing—and his trauma reaction to a patient wasn't it.

Sofia's eyes rounded, her lips parting without

a sound escaping her throat. His gaze dipped to her throat, and a smirk spread over his lips as he watched it bob.

'I was looking through the window to see what the crowd was staring at. I certainly wasn't looking *at* you. You just happened to be there,' she replied. 'I'm glad you found your shirt again.' The last words came out in a breathy tone, and she pressed her lips together.

He'd caught her off guard. Perfect. 'So you noticed I wasn't wearing one before. Did you enjoy what you saw?'

Carlos hadn't been so brazen with a woman since he'd met his late wife. Something deep inside of him unfurled as a warm caramel glow bloomed on her cheeks, the blush deepening her skin tone. There was no way she'd admit it, but the reaction told him enough. The feeling of attraction was *definitely* mutual.

'I did. The exercise was fascinating, and I've never seen anything like it before,' she replied, pushing her chin forward as she decided to purposefully misinterpret his question.

'It's called capoeira—a discipline of martial arts that combines fighting moves with music and acrobatics,' he said, daring to take a step closer into her space.

Sofia squared her shoulders as she tilted her head up to maintain eye contact, but she didn't step back. He could see the thoughts swirling behind her eyes as she calculated how good an idea it was to give in to the attraction zapping between them in electric jolts.

He was asking himself the same question, but desire had overwritten any of his objections at this point. What was the harm in giving in a little bit if he would be leaving Argentina at the end of the month?

'Have you been practicing for long?' she asked, and the fire in his veins flared at the strain in her voice. She was trying so hard to resist this moment brewing between them.

'Almost all my life.' Carlos took another step, now close enough to her that the memories of their embrace became a tangible sensation on his skin. 'I can tell you more about it over dinner. Maybe go to my place after to show you some moves…'

He wasn't sure she would accept his invitation straight away. But he wasn't trying to get her to say yes right now. Carlos was merely planting a seed—a possibility of what they could do together if they were on the same page.

So he wasn't quite prepared when Sofia bit her lower lip and asked, 'Where do want to take me?'

CHAPTER FIVE

SOFIA PATTED DOWN the fabric of her dress as she stood in front of the doors of the restaurant. The horizon had turned a dark shade of red, mixing with purple as the sun disappeared over the smooth edges of buildings dotting the skyline. Her hands had been fiddling with the flared skirt of her dress, arranging and rearranging how the folds fell while trying to get out of her head and back into the moment.

Now, several hours after Carlos had invited her to dinner with him, she was questioning the desire that had led her to say yes. Over the last week, Carlos had become the symbol for a type of adventure that had been missing from her life. One where she forgot about being cautious and letting herself live a little. Sofia *wanted* to indulge in some no-strings-attached closeness, had realised she'd wanted that ever since the tension between her and Carlos had snapped into place.

When he had brazenly invited her to his place,

she knew he was interested, too. She just needed to be brave enough to seize the opportunity.

She'd finally got him to acknowledge what had happened in the supply closet, though the conversation had not turned out the way she had expected—considering she now stood in front of a restaurant with butterflies rioting in her stomach. Instead of talking about his struggles, they had somehow ended up in a flirtatious exchange that still made her blush now. Over the last few hours, she had contemplated declining the invitation to dinner. Whatever brazen energy she had channelled had seeped out of her body. Yet there was a part of her that desperately wanted to see where this would go, even though Sofia knew it couldn't go very far. Not with him leaving and with her own lack of interest in anything emotional.

But in the short two-week span that she had now known Carlos, she had seen so many different sides of him, and what she *really* wanted was to uncover the next one. To see what else lay beneath the handsome, talented surgeon.

Sofia snapped out of her thoughts when a group of people brushed past her to enter the restaurant. Taking that as a sign from the universe wanting her to proceed, she stepped through the doors, and they swung shut behind her. The noise of the busy high street of Buenos Aires was shut out by the thick glass, the sound replaced by the murmurs of conversation and clinking of glasses and plates.

The interior of the restaurant was dimly lit, making it hard to recognise individual faces. Her eyes drifted over groups of people, not catching on to any familiar features until her eyes collided with a dark stare at the back of her room. He kept his gaze on hers for a second. Then his lids dipped low as his eyes raked over her. Awareness sprang alive within her even from this distance. The fit of the dress suddenly felt particularly snug, with the dark red fabric clinging to her torso like a second skin and only flaring out at the hips into a playful skirt.

Even from here she could see Carlos's jaw tighten as his eyes came back up. Sofia had picked out that dress for a specific purpose—to show off her body in ways she hadn't for quite some time. She had *wanted* that reaction from him, yet her heart still leapt into her throat.

Nodding at the waiter approaching her, Sofia pointed towards the table with a smile and then walked over to where Carlos was waiting. He stood up to greet her, his tall frame towering over her a considerable way. Sofia suppressed a shiver when he lay a hand on her waist and pulled her closer to brush a kiss onto her cheek.

'You look stunning, but I have a feeling you already know that,' he whispered against her ear.

A semi-circular cushioned bench wound itself around the round table, creating a more intimate setting than the traditional table and chair setups she saw throughout the restaurant. Along with the mellow scent of spices in the air and the dim lights, she wondered if anyone would even notice them…and if Carlos had picked this spot for exactly that reason.

'Thank you,' she said with a smile, watching him as he slid onto the cushioned bench. 'So do you.'

That felt like an understatement. He had changed out of the loose-fitting linen trousers and put on dark chinos instead, along with a dark purple button-up shirt. The upper two buttons were undone, giving her a hint of the dark brown skin that lay underneath. Not that she needed any hints when she'd seen him shirtless earlier today.

'Have you been here before?' she asked as she slid onto the bench on the other side of the table.

'No, but the *mestre* of the capoeira group I joined here recommended it to me,' he replied while handing her the drink menu lying flat on the table.

'Your…*maestro*?' Sofia reached for the word that sounded the most like the one he'd said, tilting her head to the side to emphasise her confusion.

'Yes, the leader of the capoeira group. He's lived in the city all his life, and he's been kind enough to suggest things I might like to do.'

The waiter stopped by their table, and they placed their order for drinks. With the drinks menu out of her hands, Sofia picked up the one for food, scanning each page. 'So, how did this recommendation come up? Did you ask for the best Asian fusion restaurant?'

The slow smile he gave her sent a spark flying down her spine. 'I asked him where he would take a beautiful woman to impress her,' he replied, his voice low and smoky.

Heat crawled up her neck and onto her face. This sort of flirting was outside of her comfort zone, because what was the point if it didn't lead to a relationship? Had she ever flirted with someone without having that particular goal in mind? The thought was sobering. Maybe Carlos was exactly the right antidote she needed to let loose without consequences.

She just needed to be brave enough to let herself go there.

And maybe the right way to do that was to be honest. He was here for a very specific reason as well, and what was the harm in telling him something about herself when he would be gone in a fortnight? She would never find out who he really was if she didn't give anything of herself.

'I've not been on a date in a long time. And definitely not on one that wasn't about romantic advances,' she said, her eyes darting back and forth from Carlos to the menu.

If her words set anything inside of him off, he didn't show it. No, he seemed comfortable in his own skin as he leaned back, his arm draped over the back of the bench and his head tilted towards her. His hand was close enough to her shoulder that she sensed a phantom touch if she focused enough on it.

Something Carlos seemed to notice as well. His fingers curled back towards his hands, then flattened out again in a repetitive motion. As if he wanted to touch her, but each time convinced himself he'd better not.

'Are you nervous?' he finally asked, his fingers once again stretching out and stopping just before they reached her shoulder.

She paused at the question, shrugging. 'I want to say no, but that's not entirely accurate. So let's say a little? I don't know what to expect, and I'm rarely in a position where I don't…know things.'

Carlos smiled at that, the lines around his eyes softening. 'I noticed. In all the short-term assignments I've accepted in recent years, I've never had quite such a vocal critique,' he said, though his tone was friendly rather than cold, as she would have expected.

Despite that, she couldn't fight the blush from deepening on her cheeks. 'I...' Her voice trailed off, and Carlos shook his head with a laugh.

'I'm not being unkind, but rather...appreciative. When you become a figure of authority in your field, people tend to take your words as the unmovable truth. Having people challenge me helps me to keep my skills sharp. Though I have to admit I can be a bit...short when challenged.' He cleared his throat as he reached for the glass in front of him to take a sip. 'It's something I'm working on.'

The earnestness of his words was so disarming and genuine that it washed away some of the nerves. Sofia may have never gone down the road of a one-night stand, but what if she didn't treat it as such and just saw what happened between them? Questions about his panic attack bubbled up inside her chest, but she swallowed them one after another. He had acknowledged what had happened earlier without going into any more details. Was she really entitled to them? Even though concern was her main motivator for asking, she couldn't push him to share more. Maybe if she let him see a piece of her, he would feel comfortable enough to share pieces of himself in return.

'I may have been a bit overprotective myself. I've spent all my senior career at Hospital General, so new things can be scary. But I'm…keen to learn from you.' In more than one way, she thought, though she didn't dare to say that out loud.

The aura around Sofia changed as their conversation went on. Shoulders that had been drawn up high slumped down, the tight smile relaxing into something small and genuine as they worked through their animosity anecdote by anecdote. As they reached the end of their main course, they'd arrived at their first surgery together, when Sofia had turned up late.

'I just can't believe you would yell at me like that in front of *my* staff,' Sofia said, with no sharpness to her words. 'And I also can't believe I apparently find that hot.'

He laughed. 'I meant it when I apologised to you. That you seem to find my lack of decorum hot says more about you than me.' They had reached a point where they could admit their shortcomings to each other, and Carlos was aware that, on his part, some of it had to do with the swirling tension of attraction between them. He *wanted* this evening to end at his place, couldn't fight the heat spreading below his skin and pooling in his stomach.

'I can't really explain any of…this.' Sofia pointed between them with a raised eyebrow, her lips curving into a smile that he wanted to kiss right off her face. The urge to touch her was a steady beat inside of him, and he knew he would succumb to it soon. Especially since she'd been getting closer to him throughout their dinner, the distance between them growing ever smaller.

'Then again, I'm not one to be casual,' she added, stopping his thoughts in their tracks.

Neither was he, though the reply wouldn't cross his lips. From the moment he'd asked her to dinner, a part of him had worried about the conversation becoming too personal. Though she might be the first person since Rosa to inspire attraction within him, he wasn't in a place where he could share those thoughts. He doubted that he would ever reach that kind of closure.

But despite knowing that, he couldn't stop himself from feeling the draw towards her.

His hand unfurled, his fingers winding through her hair until he made contact with the back of her neck. Cradling her head, he leaned into her space as he asked, 'What was your last relationship like if it wasn't casual?'

The spark in her eyes dimmed, and something inside him twisted. There was a hint of pain that might be too personal for the thing they wanted to start between them, but he wanted to know where it came from anyway.

'I've had bad luck finding the right person who fits into my life,' she said, her voice quieter than usual. 'With the work we do, it's not easy to find someone who will understand that sometimes I can't just leave work at the hospital. My relationships ended because they couldn't get the level of commitment they wanted from me, and that was fine by me. I've put my career as a surgeon above anything else.'

She paused, her eyes gliding away from his face to grab her glass. Her fingers trailed over the rim of it in a wide circle, and he dropped his eyes to watch the movement.

Carlos sensed there was a particular person she was thinking of, but forced himself not to pry. He didn't understand why he wanted to get to know her better, only that there was a need inside of him to uncover more of her.

'With my last boyfriend, Daniel, I'd thought things would be different. He never once complained about me cutting dates short if I was paged, or that we had to figure out plans around my schedule. Turns out he ended up being the worst of them.' Sofia took a sip of her drink, raising her eyes to him as she set the glass back down. The tingling in his fingers where they cradled her head intensified as she looked at him.

'So now I'm ready to try the casual route. That seems the logical way to get my needs met without all the messy attachment.'

Carlos took a sharp inhale when she leaned into his touch, twisting her head so his hand landed on her cheek. Like an automatic reflex, his thumb stroked over her soft skin in a slow arc. This wasn't the direction he'd expected from this conversation. The mention of her latest ex-boyfriend bothered him more than he had expected. The pain still lived within her, bubbling close enough to the surface that he guessed their breakup was recent.

Though that wasn't what was strange. No, what threw Carlos for a loop was the surge of protectiveness zapping through his chest at the thought of the wrongs this man had inflicted on Sofia. The way she spoke about her previous relationships was clinical, like she had long ago processed her feelings. But some rawness had sneaked back into her voice at the mention of Daniel.

He wanted to know how he had turned out to be the worst of them all, but bit back the question. What use would it be to know that about her?

'You sure you want this with me?' he asked instead. The skin of her cheek warmed underneath his hand, sparking a response in his own body. He knew *he* wanted this, yearned to be connected to her in a way he hadn't wanted anyone since Rosa's passing.

Was this the first sign of healing? Carlos wasn't sure he could ever open his heart to another person again, but Sofia reached something within him he'd kept hidden away from everyone. She wasn't afraid to challenge him and, with that simple action, somehow saw beyond the walls he'd raised. It had been enough to bring to life the warmth of attraction.

'As long as we both want the same thing. I might not be experienced in no-strings-attached arrangements, but I know I don't want more than that.' Sofia paused, as if she was listening back to her own words, then extended her hand until it lay splayed on his chest.

The touch sent a current of electricity through him, and her fingers dug into the fabric of his shirt as his chest expanded with a deep breath. His thumb stopped its arc over her cheek, and his hand wandered down to her chin. At the slightest pressure from him, she tilted it upwards, and Carlos's eyes dipped lower, watching her pulse beat against the base of her neck.

He imagined—not for the first time—what she would taste like there, and this time, he didn't fight the urge. He let himself sink into the fantasy and lowered his head to press it against her collarbone.

Above him Sofia gasped, and that small sound was enough to drive his heated blood to the lower half of his body. He paused for a second, composing himself before he whispered onto her skin, 'This is so much better than I imagined.'

Another small sound escaped her mouth when his lips trailed along her jaw. He stopped when he reached her ear and took her earlobe between his teeth as he breathed in. Her scent was intoxicating, filling his head with even more fantasies than he'd been indulging in since their first encounter in the OR.

But before they went any further, he needed to be clear with her. 'I don't get personal with anyone in my life,' he said simply as he drew back to look at her. The glaze over her eyes filled him with regret that they hadn't had the conversation earlier. But if she agreed to come with him now, she needed to know this about him. So he continued, 'The reason I move around a lot is because I don't like to get to know people, and I don't tend to answer personal questions.'

Sofia blinked, slowly, and he wondered if she was struggling with the same restraint he was. Or was what he'd said somehow too much for her? But then she nodded while lifting one shoulder in a shrug. 'Will you still tell me about how you learned to move like that with capoeira?'

He smiled at her words, and his lips closed

around her earlobe again before he drew back and angled his mouth over hers. He held her gaze as their noses touched, searching them for a hint of hesitation or second thoughts. All he found in them was a curious spark that lit a flame of hunger he recognised all too well.

Her lashes lowered when he nudged her nose with his, and a shaky breath escaped her throat. Her hand burrowed deeper into his shirt. When she pulled him closer to her, Carlos huffed out a laugh before giving in to his own desire.

Their lips met in a tender, tentative kiss that instantly felt familiar—like he'd been waiting for these exact lips all his life. The silky feel of them engulfed him, washed through his body in a wave of heat and sparks. His hands came up to her face, pulling her closer. He eased her head back to deepen the kiss, and a soft moan drifted to his ear from her throat.

That small sound was enough to drive him over the edge. He rode the rising tide of desire in his body, and forgot that he had ever meant to be cautious around her. All he could think of was how badly he wanted to have her underneath him and wring every drop of pleasure out of her.

Carlos knew he shouldn't. Knew that even if she agreed to go home with him tonight, it would be all about her pleasure. For the last five years, he had not thought about sleeping with anyone and had truly believed that part of his life over. Considered it part of his penance for letting Rosa down. So as far as protection was concerned, he wasn't…prepared. But that wouldn't stop him from getting a taste right now.

If Sofia agreed.

Her tongue swiped over his lips, begging him for entrance that he wanted to grant her. But he forced himself to pull back, leaning his forehead against hers to look at her.

'Instead of telling you how I learned to move like that, how about I show you?' he said, a smile tugging at his lips as he looked at her puffy lips and passion-glazed eyes.

Her throat bobbed, and it took her a moment to catch her breath. His heart skipped a beat when she asked, 'Where do you live?'

CHAPTER SIX

WHEN SOFIA HAD entered the restaurant earlier in the evening, she had not expected to end up at Carlos's place. Then again, when she had left the hospital after her shift, she also hadn't thought she would have dinner with the man she had until fairly recently considered her arch-nemesis.

Despite her question, she knew there was only one reason why Carlos had invited her to his place, and it had precious little to do with explaining capoeira to her. That was clear from the kiss they'd shared. The phantom sensation of his lips on her collarbone still danced over her skin, sending shivers of need through her body down into her core.

As she stepped into the elevator to his flat with his warm hand on the small of her back, she realised—with not a small amount of shock—how much she had wanted this from the moment they met. The tension from their disagreements at work had led to this situation, turning their dislike into a searing-hot attraction that had resulted in the invitation to his place.

Was that what he wanted from her? A quick fling with all the fun and none of the commitment? Judging by the fire in his eyes, he wanted to devour her right here on the spot. And that thought sent more sparks flying through her body in uncontrollable arcs.

Sofia had never considered acting on attraction without emotion and the firm boundaries of a relationship. But maybe that was the way busy surgeons like themselves were supposed to do it?

Would someone as experienced as Carlos be turned off by her lack of knowledge? Though she had been the one to talk about her relationships—and about not wanting one—the way his lips trailing over her skin had her clenching around nothing convinced her of his prowess as a lover.

But then she'd gone ahead and mentioned Daniel. She had only shared a sliver of her experience with him, but she'd seen Carlos's eyes shutter for a moment, as if put off. And a few moments later, Sofia had understood why. He didn't do personal. All he wanted was to come to an agreement and enjoy her companionship without any of her baggage.

That was what she wanted as well, right? It

shouldn't bother her that she would never get an answer to the questions about him that were still bubbling up inside of her.

'What's going on? I think I lost you there for a second.' Carlos's words snapped her back to reality, and she looked at the open elevator door. His hand was placed on the sensor of the door, preventing it from closing as he looked at her.

'Sorry, I was just in my head. It's been a while since I've been with anyone...'

A nervous laugh bubbled up in her chest as she stepped into the elevator, and she immediately regretted her words. He didn't want to know anything about her. His interest in her was purely physical, and she needed to remember that. Before long, the fire in her veins would bank until it vanished along with Carlos.

'Tell me about what happened the last time you did,' he said as he followed her into the elevator, his voice still low enough to raise the hairs on the back of her neck.

Carlos took out a key fob from the messenger bag hanging around his shoulder and swiped it over a reader at the bottom of the number panel. The doors closed with a soft thud. Then the elevator moved up. Sofia watched as the numbers went by until they passed twenty and the display changed to *P*.

The doors opened and revealed a panoramic view of Buenos Aires's night-time skyline. The entire wall consisted of tall windows, the moon and starlight the only thing illuminating her surroundings. A modern kitchen opened up to her left, its black marble countertops gleaming in the dying light, and in front of the windows was a couch large enough to seat an entire surgical team.

'You live in a penthouse?' Sofia asked as she stepped closer to the windows to look at the view. 'Damn, I'm going to talk to our boss about getting a raise.'

Carlos stepped up behind her as she peered through the windows and took in the skyline of Buenos Aires. His chest was close enough to her back to touch it, but he deliberately kept a few centimetres of distance between them—or at least she thought it to be deliberate. If she let herself lean back just a little, she would get that touch her insides were screaming for.

'This penthouse is up for sale, and they rent it out for short-term arrangements while they're looking for a buyer,' he said, his voice so close that each word sent a rush of breath over her skin.

'Still has to cost you a pretty penny. And you don't even get to enjoy it because you spend all your time at the hospital.' Sofia dared to shoot him a look over her shoulder. A shiver skittered down her spine as her eyes locked onto his, the hunger she beheld in them stoking the flame in her core to new heights.

'How long is "a while"?' Carlos asked.

'What?' She didn't know what else to say to his question.

'You said you haven't been with anyone "in a while".'

Her heart leapt into her throat as the words dropped into her consciousness like they were weighed down with stones. She spun around to face him, her eyes drawn to his lips, which were curled in a slight smile. The memory of what it felt like to have his mouth pressed against hers sent another surge of heat through her.

Was he suddenly concerned about her level of experience?

'Does it matter? I thought you didn't want to do personal questions.'

Carlos's gaze roamed up and down her body as he stepped closer, causing shivers wherever his eyes went. There was an assessing quality to the sweep of his gaze, but she didn't feel exposed like she thought she would. No, what he awakened inside of her was the raging fury of desire.

'I said *I* don't want to answer personal questions. But you're right to request that rule apply to you as well. So let me ask you something else instead.' Her back hit the cool glass behind her when he took a step forward, his hand coming to rest on the window right next to her head. His head dipped down, finding the hollow of her collarbone. The open-mouthed kiss he pressed onto it shot lightning through her. 'I know what I want from you. But what do *you* want, Sofia?'

Her mouth went dry at the question she'd been asking herself.

There was no denying the attraction heating the surrounding air—and it had been far too long since she and Daniel had broken up. Though their relationship had ended poorly, the sex had always been good. If his kisses were anything to go by, Carlos knew exactly what he was doing. It would be more than *just* good.

'I think we both know you didn't invite me here to show me any capoeira steps. That probably doesn't require as much kissing as we've already done. I liked it, so maybe that's a good place to start and work our way towards...' Her voice trailed off as butterflies bounced in her stomach, throwing her off.

Carlos huffed out a low laugh that skittered across her skin. 'Kissing you hadn't been the plan when I followed you earlier today, but I'm happy to be here with you.'

He paused, his other hand coming down on the glass so that her head was now boxed in between his arms—making her shiver. Her clothes lay heavy on her skin, fraying her nerves wherever they made contact with her, and she was sure if he were to lean in now to eliminate the remaining space between their lips, she would combust.

'So, you want to sleep with me?' He leaned in slightly closer with each word, his lips hovering over hers with a tantalising proximity that made her squirm underneath his gaze.

'Yes.' Sofia let the truth of her intentions shine through this one word. The cautious part in her wanted to decline—to leave and pretend like nothing had ever happened between them. But it was also the cautious part that had led her into relationships that were doomed to fail. All because she understood the parameters of a romantic relationship, understood her expectations and responsibilities. That was how she had been taught things should be—books, TV shows, her own parents. They all had shown her that there was only one way to have a man in her life.

But what if that concept simply didn't fit into her life, and some closeness here and there when it presented itself was what she was actually looking for? The way Carlos led his life.

Shaking off the last vestiges of hesitation, Sofia let her hands come to rest on his chest, feeling the hardness of his pecs as she dug her fingers into the fabric of his shirt. 'We both know this isn't anything serious. We're simply getting rid of the tension at work in a creative way.'

Sofia already suspected that Carlos wasn't interested in anything romantic either, but she still wasn't prepared for his expression shuttering. It was only for a second, enough to notice, but not enough to understand what was going through his head. A heartbeat passed and then the smile was back, lips curved in an expression of pure seduction.

'I'm leaving Buenos Aires in two weeks. Casual is all I'm looking for,' he said, and Sofia ignored the thing twisting in her chest.

She might have never had a casual encounter before, but that didn't mean she needed to attach needless emotions to what was happening here. It was good that he wasn't looking for anything serious. Neither was she. Her serious relationships, the ones that were by the book, they had all ended in heartbreak. Maybe it was time to paint outside the lines for once.

A surge of renewed confidence emboldened her. She slipped her hands to his back and pulled him closer so his chest lay flush against hers. Then she angled her head up to meet his gaze, putting all her intentions into her eyes, hoping he understood. Carlos did, for the small smile unfurled into something larger and hungrier, and her lids fluttered closed when his mouth finally dipped down to capture her lips.

Her lips were soft against his, the touch filled with more passion and heat than their first kiss at the restaurant. Every single nerve ending in his body was blazing, his skin alight with an invisible fire that burst free from a place he'd long since hidden away from the public. A place Sofia had found and was now standing in front of, trying to figure out how to climb the wall she had encountered.

Or at least that's what the withdrawn part of his brain wanted him to believe—while the part that was starved for touch was ready to let go right this second. Just tonight—and the pleasure would be only hers. Even if he wanted to, he couldn't give more today.

His desire for her wasn't wrong, was it? He wasn't dishonouring Rosa's memory by finally giving in to something he had yearned for? This wasn't about finding a new wife or forgetting what he had done in the past. No, he would carry the scars and the guilt over it with him for the rest of his life. Nobody could erase that.

But Carlos couldn't deny what this kiss was doing to him—that something inside of him was coming undone. Sofia had found him in a place no one else ever had, and though he had sensed

the undercurrent of attraction in all of their inter-
actions, it wasn't until his most vulnerable moment that his view had changed. As though her
talking him down from his panic had left a sliver
of him open to her. It was the only explanation
that made sense to him for why he wanted Sofia
as much as he did. How she was the first person
to reach him again on any level.

He pressed her further into the glass behind
her as their lips moved together, and everything
inside him clenched when a muffled moan escaped her throat. He'd forgotten what it was like
to be wanted. The ghost of it had visited him during their last encounter, when she had embraced
him. The memory was foggy, tainted by the sheer
panic he'd been trying to control, but the spark
had been there in the moment—trying to break
through. His lips had skittered over the sensitive
skin of her neck, brushing over her earlobe, and
the sound she had made then...

Carlos hardened at the memory. He needed to
hear that sound again now.

His hands slipped away from where they rested
on the glass, coming down on Sofia's hips and
pulling her closer to him. His lips remained fused
to hers, their kiss a dance of teeth and tongues as
they deepened their connection. All the while, his
fingers moved down her sides, finding the hem

of her dress and slipping underneath to feel the bare skin of her thighs.

Another muffled moan came from her throat, and Carlos was certain he would shatter if she did it again. His skin was already impossibly tight from the repressed desire surging forward. He had denied himself all this for the last five years, thinking even casual encounters a betrayal of the promises he'd made—and the promises he had broken. What had changed inside him that he was willing to let loose in this moment? Carlos didn't know, but that would be something to explore later.

Sofia demanded all his attention.

His mouth left hers to explore more of her again. A shudder raked through him as he tasted the skin of her neck, the memory of their first kiss in the restaurant radiating through him with a searing heat. She let out a small huff every time his lips connected with her flesh, and her pleasure at his touch brought a primal satisfaction to his chest that he hadn't felt in ages. It only heightened his own desire.

Her enthusiastic response had him eagerly continuing his exploration, his hands moving over her clothed torso and dipping behind, where he found her zipper. He paused there to give Sofia the chance to withdraw or speak up. When she surged forward to press her mouth against his again, he dragged the zipper down.

The fabric fell from her shoulders, revealing centimetre after delicious centimetre of caramel flesh. He bowed his head, feathering kisses onto her skin as he peeled the dress down her body. His hands moved up her sides, relishing the feel of velvety skin. Then he paused, fully enraptured by the sight of her bared to his gaze. Her curves looked as soft as they felt, the gentle slope of her hips narrowing as he traced the line up to her waist and then flaring out again as her torso expanded.

'I see you came here prepared,' he said with a huffed laugh, and watched with way too much male satisfaction as a blush deepened the hue of the skin on her cheeks.

'Bold of you to assume I'm not wearing a bra just because of you,' she said, pushing her chin out in a now familiar gesture of challenge that he'd observed her throwing at him many times at the hospital.

Carlos decided to play along, looking at her with feigned surprise. 'You're saying this is not for me?'

Before she could answer, he ran his hands back up her body and palmed both her breasts.

The skin was soft and heated against his hand, and when his thumb lightly stroked over her nipple, she arched her back, pushing further into his touch. Renewed desire thundered through him, so strong and savage that he had to take a few steadying breaths. Because he had denied himself the company of a woman for so long, the onslaught of sensation was threatening to overwhelm him. Carlos wasn't allowed to let that happen. He *wanted* this to last as long as possible, taking his time to acquaint himself with every part of her body.

His face dipped below her jawline, his lips brushing over her neck, then wandering lower still. His mouth watered as he hovered in front of her breast. So many things popped into his mind that he wanted to do to her. Tentatively, both to tease and to test the water, he extended his tongue far enough for its tip to just whisper over her nipple.

The response was instant. A soft cry escaped her lips, her muscles under his hands tensing and releasing as pleasure speared through her. He smiled to himself, his own need growing— a fact he knew was apparent by just looking at him. But that wasn't what this night was about. It would only be about her.

When he closed his whole mouth around the tip of her breast and sucked, Sofia's whimper turned into a low moan. Her hands came down on his shoulders, gripping at the fabric there and pulling his shirt up. Whether it was on purpose or because she needed something to hang on to, Carlos didn't know, but he let her pull the buttons apart before flinging the shirt off his shoulders.

He rested his forehead on her sternum as he pulled her closer again, his nose brushing the sensitive skin between her breasts. There he inhaled deeply, her scent sending lightning strikes through his body.

'You smell delicious,' he said, letting the thought out without considering what he was saying. 'I can't wait to find out what you taste like.'

He kissed each breast to underline his words, his tongue briefly swirling around each peaked nipple. Then he shot up, standing tall in front of her, and his eyes narrowed on her with a smile. 'Hold on tight,' he said as he wrapped his arms around her and lifted her off the floor to carry her to the couch behind them.

Sofia yelped as her feet lost contact with the floor. She pushed her hips into his erection as she wrapped her legs around his waist. Carlos hissed at the sudden pressure, his restraint already stretched to near maximum. It would be *very* hard to stop at this point, but he hadn't expected this. He wasn't…prepared. But he couldn't let this end before he knew what she tasted like.

The fabric of the couch was cool against her skin, and Sofia took in a shaky breath. Everything within her was taut and loose at the same time, her body reacting to Carlos's touch in ways she hadn't expected. If she had thought earlier that the sex she'd had in the past was good, she needed to revise that statement.

This was good, and they hadn't even arrived at the main event. Whatever she had experienced in the past paled in comparison—it wasn't even a contest.

Her mind had completely emptied of everything when Carlos climbed on top of her with a smile that let her see all of his primal intentions for her. Intentions that had her squeezing her thighs together to seek relief in what little friction she could manage like that.

Carlos noticed the tensing of her muscles, for his smile grew into a grin.

'Impatient, are we?' he drawled, and Sofia raised her head to look at him.

Whatever she had intended to retort died in her throat, turning into a low moan when his hands dipped beneath the skirt of her dress and pulled it down, leaving her in nothing but her underwear. When his hands brushed over her wet panties, her head lolled back as a strike of electricity shook her body.

Carlos positioned himself between her legs while kneeling on the floor. Lying flat on the couch, she couldn't see him, but his breath against her skin had her imagination running wild, her body tensing with anticipation—and a dose of fear at the lack of control.

This wasn't a position Sofia was used to. Her entire life was built around the concept of controlling what she could and adapting to the things she couldn't. That was the working principle of trauma surgery, after all. It was how she operated in her relationships as well, taking charge and setting the expectations from the very beginning.

She hadn't done any of that with Carlos, had relinquished so much of her ability to control things to him—trusting him to do that. Where was she taking this trust from? She knew him to be a capable doctor and a surgeon with a level of skill she dreamed about attaining some day. But did she know enough about him to just…let him do things his way?

The thought kept coming back as she tried to push it away and stay in the moment with him. She knew she *wanted* him to continue. Her body's response to his touch was evidence enough. Why was her brain suddenly trying to ruin a good thing for her?

A ripple of pleasure dispelled some of the tension building in her muscles when Carlos brushed his fingers along the hem of her underwear. Then she gasped as his thumb stroked her through the silken fabric, the current of lightning intensifying. She was enjoying his touch way too much, and small bubbles of doubt kept surfacing in her mind when she would rather focus on the moment.

How Carlos had noticed what was going on inside her head she didn't know, but his fingers suddenly stopped their tender caress. He looked up to meet her gaze.

'You're not used to a man pleasuring you?' he asked, his tone curious rather than critical as she had expected.

Sofia swallowed the lump in her throat. A part of her wanted to deny it, yearned to appear as experienced as he clearly was. But the softness in his expression, the complete lack of judgement she saw in his eyes—it coaxed her into a feeling of safety. So she nodded and said, 'I'm usually the person setting the pace.'

Carlos sat up, a thoughtful expression bunching up his brows. His eyes darted around the couch. Then he stood, gathering two large pillows from the opposite ends. Leaning over her with a soft smile, he pulled her into a sitting position by her hands, then placed the cushions behind her before pushing her back down.

He kissed her, and her lips immediately opened for his. A deep moan released from her chest as their tongues tangled, her stomach swooping as if she were weightless. The air between them sparked when he severed their connection, and Carlos wound his way down her body, stopping here and there to kiss, nip and suck at his leisure before settling back down between her thighs, his knees on the floor again.

Her heart squeezed when she realised what he had done. With her head now elevated by the cushions, she could see *everything* he was doing. Not only had he understood where her hesitation was coming from without her having to explain, he had also found a solution for her.

As if he was reading her mind, Carlos said, 'You're in control here. You see something you don't like, just hit me in the back of the head.'

Sofia couldn't help but laugh at that. The image his words conjured in her mind was so different from the situation they were in. 'I think I'll just tell you to stop,' she said with a chuckle, and with each breath, whatever tension she had been carrying flowed out of her body.

'I guess that works, too.' He smirked before he dropped his gaze, and his eyes turned entirely feral again.

His fingers resumed their exploration, finding each spot of sensitive skin with precision. Not only had he known what she needed on an emotional level right now, but apparently he also knew exactly how to touch her in a way she had never experienced before. That she was able to watch him skim his fingers over her, her wetness leaving traces on him even through the silken fabric of her panties, only heightened the delicious torture he was inflicting on her.

When another searing spear of need lanced through her from his slow and deliberate touches, she bucked her hips—to urge him on.

Carlos chuckled. 'You really are incredibly impatient, sweetheart,' he said, his face so close to her flesh that she felt his hot breath grazing her.

'If I can tell you to stop, I can probably also tell you to go ahead?' Sofia asked, knowing the answer even before she saw the eager gleam in his eyes.

'There's nothing hotter than a woman telling me what she wants me to do to her.' His voice was akin to a growl, his tone so low that another wave of need rushed to her core. She moved her hips again, bringing her closer to his face.

Sofia gasped when his lips made contact with the sensitive skin at the top of her leg and then wandered down. He hooked his finger underneath the front of her panties, and his breath hit the flesh underneath as he bent down.

'This is everything I've been thinking about for the last week,' he whispered, each word creating another huff of air that skittered over her skin.

He didn't give Sofia the chance to reply. Instead, Carlos lowered his head and put his mouth to her, his tongue parting her folds in one lazy and smooth stroke that turned her gasps of anticipation into a delighted groan.

Every muscle inside of her loosened at the feel of his lips against her, the intimate caress demanding all of her attention. A ball of tension bounced around in the pit of her stomach—higher and higher with each lick and stroke from Carlos until stars began to drift in front of her eyes. She wanted to watch him, the view of this gorgeous man between her legs adding to the pleasure of what he was doing. But the sensations were too much, and she let her lids close as she gave herself to the sensation mounting within her.

Sofia thought it couldn't get any more intense—until his fingers joined his mouth. He pushed into her. The light of the stars burst alive, blinding her as pure ecstasy flooded her system.

'Right there, right there.' She heard these words over and over, pushing through the haze of bliss enveloping her and grabbing her attention. Then the tension in her stomach crested, firing her down the starlit corridor in a crash landing that turned into a long, drawn-out moan—and had her realising she had been the one urging him on.

Heat flooded her cheeks as the high of her orgasm trickled through her, reality slowly creeping back in. Carlos kissed her thighs gently, the tip of his tongue darting out now and then as he made his way back up her body. His erection settled against her, and her body reacted instantly.

Carlos let out a sound that was half chuckle, half groan as he bent down and pulled her into a kiss. She wrapped her arms around him, her fingers dancing over his back as they found their way down. But when she pushed her fingers below his waistband, he broke the kiss and looked at her.

The fire in his eyes matched the roaring flames underneath her skin, yet there was something else in them. A tiny sliver of regret.

'I have a confession to make, sweetheart,' he said, and the muscles that had been loose from her post-orgasmic bliss tensed up.

Carlos sensed it and immediately bent down to breathe another kiss onto her lips. 'Nothing catastrophic, don't panic. More a selfishness on my part.' His lips trailed over her cheek and down her neck, summoning the fog of lust around her brain. 'I know you can feel how much I want you, but I'm not prepared yet.'

'Prepared?' Sofia asked, trying to focus on his words while the path of his lips caused shivers to rake through her body.

'I don't have any protection to make sure we are both safe going any further than this,' he replied, and the haziness enveloping her dispersed.

'You don't?' The question came out a lot more

incredulous than she intended. Carlos seemed to have picked up on that, for he stopped the wandering of his mouth to look at her.

'I'm not in the habit of taking a box of condoms with me whenever I travel for work.' There was an edge to his voice. Sofia knew she hadn't caused him any offence with her question, but she had inevitably poked at something she hadn't meant to.

He didn't travel with condoms? For some reason, that thought was hard for her to reconcile with the image of Carlos she had constructed in her head. Didn't he have a different lover in every single hospital he worked at? Wasn't that what he wanted from her?

'Right… This isn't actually your home. Sorry,' she said, not wanting to spoil the mood further by doubling down on her incredulity.

That seemed to be enough to take him off guard. Carlos shifted his weight off her to lie next to her, his hand splayed on her stomach and drawing gentle circles as he looked at her. 'I had to have a taste—even though I knew that was as far as we could go with things. You are just so… delicious.'

A swarm of butterflies burst alive in the pit of her stomach at his words, and a nervous giggle climbed up her throat. 'You're sweet to say that,' she said, the lack of creativity in her words making her cringe. Was there a more boring person on the planet? If only there was a rulebook on how to speak to a casual lover—that would be her salvation. Because she didn't even know how to be interesting enough to prevent a guy from cheating on her. Things got infinitely more complicated if she considered the dynamic between her and Carlos.

'Just the facts,' he said as he raised one shoulder, his fingers still tracing over her exposed skin, drawing attention to her nakedness.

What was the protocol post-climax? Was she supposed to leave straight away? Was there a certain amount of small talk before they went about their day? God, why was she so bad with men? No wonder Daniel did what he did when she couldn't even navigate this casual interaction with Carlos.

'What's wrong?' Carlos's question pierced through the whirlwind of insecurities rising in her thoughts. He must have sensed her tensing, or how else would he know what was going on in her mind?

Lacking any kind of excuse or experience to fall back on, Sofia decided to go with the truth. 'I've never done this before.'

A line appeared between his brows as he considered her, confusion rippling over his face. He leaned away from her. 'This as in...*this*?' His hand splayed out again, pressing gently down on her stomach to indicate her.

She immediately shook her head as she realised what he had misunderstood. 'No, I've had sex. I realise I said it before, but I don't really know how to navigate…this kind of casual interaction.'

Carlos relaxed back against her, his fingers resuming their gentle caress as he looked at her. His expression softened, letting her glimpse the man behind the typical surgeon bravado she'd observed in most of her colleagues—herself included. Something lay beneath the surface, something that remained hidden away and might burst into flames if the light of day touched it. A fragile piece of himself that was coming out now as they lay entangled in each other with only half their clothes on.

Sofia had seen the other side of that vulnerability before, when she had grounded him through his panic attack.

His lips parted as if he was going to say something, but then the vulnerable spark died in his eyes. His fingers wandered up her torso, grazing over the underside of her breast. For a fraction of a second, Sofia got the sense that somehow sex with her was an escape for him—though she couldn't even begin to understand what he would be escaping from. Or where that suspicion even came from.

But then his knuckles brushed over her taut nipple, sending a renewed wave of pleasure through her body. 'We make the rules here. Whenever you have a question or a concern, just tell me,' he said, bending down to brush his lips against hers. 'Now I really have to shower. I'm usually one to wash up before doing anything, but you were just so…'

The memory of how everything had started came back to her, and Sofia laughed as Carlos got to his feet. 'You never got to show me what capoeira actually is,' she said, her eyes gliding over his muscled back.

A hum of appreciation escaped her throat, and Carlos looked back at her. 'Next time,' he said, winking.

Then he caught her off guard again when he tucked each thumb under his waistband and pushed his trousers and underwear down, filling in the blanks in her imagination. Before she could say anything, he reached his hand towards her and curled his fingers, beckoning. 'You want to join me in the shower? There are a lot of things we can do that don't require protection.'

CHAPTER SEVEN

CARLOS WATCHED WITH a satisfied nod as the junior surgeons wheeled the patient out of the OR. With his third week beginning today, he now let the trained staff guide the surgery and take the lead on most of it. They had put the surgical plan together on the fly and needed very little guidance on what to do if they encountered obstacles. An observation Carlos was pleased with. He'd spent many hours in the operating room and during rounds teaching his triage technique and had them memorise it, practicing it on made-up scenarios over and over until they could triage a patient in their sleep.

The effort had paid off. They could now fall back on his teachings in emergency surgery, remembering what was critical and what could wait. All the staff had responded well to his guidance, and he knew he would spend the rest of his contract observing and course-correcting.

The lightness of a job well done filled him. Of course, he knew if he looked closer, that wasn't the only thing uplifting his mood—though he didn't dare to think too hard about what else there was. Sofia's draw on him was already overwhelming his senses.

Her taste still clung to his lips days later, the feel of her mouth around him a thrilling sensation that had kept him awake at night with an aching need only she could fulfil. Stepping into the shower to start his day had brought back the memories of their night together, and Carlos had almost grabbed Sofia and pulled her into what he now considered their closet when she gave him a secretive wink earlier today.

Though he had enjoyed the attention of different women over the last five years, he had never let it go anywhere beyond the occasional flirtation. The walls around him were too high to let anyone come close enough, even just for casual sex.

But Sofia had seen him in a vulnerable position, had sensed his panic on her own skin, and had remained there with him until he had calmed down. She'd been willing to do that for someone who didn't rank much higher than a stranger—one she had daily disagreements with at work.

He wondered if that tension had translated into their explosive connection, because he didn't know what else to make of it. No one else had ever managed to interest him. The guilt set in too quickly, not even letting him consider an attachment to any woman—casual or otherwise.

Tendrils of fire licked at his insides, and Carlos did the second most impulsive thing he had done in the last three days—the first one being inviting Sofia to his place. He let the flames burn, relishing the heat they sent coursing through his body.

The guilt was ever-present, and he didn't think it would ever go away. How could he just get over how utterly he had let his late wife down? But it seemed less pressing around Sofia, giving him room to enjoy her company without suffocating.

Pushing through the door of the OR, Carlos glanced at the surgical board on the wall. Two surgeries were currently going on, but Sofia wasn't a part of either of them. He tried to remember if she had told him what she was up to today, but they hadn't spoken since they had slipped into the supply closet yesterday for a make-out session that had left them both catching their breaths—and making plans for when they would go to his place again.

There had only been a short glance exchanged between them when he went to answer a page in the ER earlier. But she had been carrying some snacks and a tablet when he'd walked past her. Chances were that she was catching up on her notes somewhere on the floor. So Carlos went around the trauma department, sticking his head into different rooms and excusing himself when he interrupted someone until he found Sofia in a small staff room, staring at the tablet while popping grapes into her mouth absent-mindedly.

Carlos cleared his throat, and Sofia's eyes only briefly left the screen as if she wasn't worried about someone interrupting her. He grinned when recognition caught up with her and she looked up again, this time with the distinct glow of a blush on her high cheekbones.

'Enjoying yourself?' he asked as he walked over to stand behind her chair. There were several centimetres of space between them, but he still felt the heat radiating from her. Or was he the one setting the air between them on fire? He couldn't tell any more, their mutual attraction taking on a life and shape of its own.

'How much fun can you have doing patient notes?' She glanced down at the notepad lying next to the keyboard, then tilted her head back to look at him.

Carlos bit his lip at that, willing his breath to come out at a steady pace. The way she gazed up at him, he could see the entire column of her throat, the caramel skin looking soft and damn near edible even in the harsh light of the hospital. Then his eyes wandered further, glancing down the front of her scrub top. The neckline gave him a hint of an enticing view.

Without thinking, he leaned forward to see more, his torso coming close enough that it connected with the back of her chair.

'Try writing some silly notes in between the serious ones. It breaks up the monotony,' he said, his voice loaded with a suggestive tone that had nothing to do with his words and everything to do with the feelings she awakened in him.

'Silly notes?' If Sofia realised what the mere sliver of her visible skin was doing to him, she chose to ignore it as she kept her eyes trained on him, one eyebrow raised.

'Yeah, like "Patient demonstrates an uncanny ability to maintain a perfect level of room noise by consistent snoring. Rhythm remains stable. Recommend noise-cancelling headphones for the night shift nurse."'

Sofia blinked at him twice. Then her lips split apart in a wide grin that turned into a laugh. The sound of her laughter filled the small room, enveloping him in a sensation that wasn't part of the flames licking at him from the inside, but it burned just as much.

'Dr Carlos Cabrera, the no-nonsense surgeon who has been hounding us all about proper triage protocols during trauma surgery, writes silly notes into his patient charts?' The amusement twinkling in her eyes had to be one of the most attractive things he'd ever seen. It shot right through him, settling down in the centre of his chest.

'I would never leave the notes in. They're just something fun to do when you feel like the admin work is never-ending—which it is,' he replied, hoping to draw another laugh from her.

But Sofia just smiled and then did something way better. She tilted her head further back so that the top of her head was now pushing against his stomach. Holding eye contact with him, she sunk her teeth into her lower lip, and the sound fighting its way out of his throat could only be described as a growl.

Without thinking, he put his hands on her shoulders. His thumbs brushed over her collarbone before lifting the fabric of her top so his fingers could slip beneath her collar. From there, he let them trail further down, brushing over the tops of her breasts.

'This is so not by the book, Carlos,' Sofia said as she huffed out a breath. Though her words were meant to admonish him, he only heard excitement in them.

'So is sleeping with your co-worker,' he replied. Then he bent down to brush his lips against her neck.

The second he had entered the room and seen her, his mind had emptied out of any other thoughts. The hesitation, the questions over whether what he was doing was appropriate, had gone…along with the heaviness of the guilt sitting on his shoulders.

There was something about Sofia that he couldn't explain, but she brought him a lightness he hadn't felt since that day five years ago. A reprieve of the constant struggle—of *having* to play by the book because going outside of the established lines had brought tragedy to his life in the first place.

In this moment—as well as all the nights spent at his place since the first time—he could just *be* without anything weighing him down. That feeling was one he hadn't felt in so many years. It was intoxicating, and he couldn't resist it. No matter how much he knew it would probably be for the best if he did.

Sofia herself had given him the best reason to pull back. She had said she had never had a casual encounter with anyone. All her experiences had been in relationships. Carlos has almost shared that he wasn't used to casual encounters, either. There had been a few wild years during his early junior years, seeking release from the stress of being a newly minted doctor in different ways. Sex was great for that.

Was it fair of him to pull her into his orbit when he knew he would be leaving in less than two weeks? That he would never be hers? She had said that was what she was looking for. But could he be sure she meant what she said when she had never had a casual affair?

'Yeah, the hospital handbook has a whole chapter dedicated to fraternisation. There are procedures in place to safeguard the hospital from any liability, and we definitely disregarded many of them many nights this week.' Her voice was low and breathy as his lips continued their caress on her neck.

'Are you ready to shed the final vestiges of your aggressively by-the-book vibes?' Carlos had enjoyed that description of her when she had first mentioned it to him, seeing a lot of himself in it. Though people like that definitely didn't come on to their colleagues the way he was doing right now when they were rule-followers.

Hadn't he himself privately criticised Sebastián for living his marriage too openly in front of the staff? The amount of information he'd heard fluttering around the corridors of the hospital about this man's marriage problems and their reconciliation had him questioning whether he had made a mistake coming to this place.

Now Carlos was the one getting inappropriately close to a co-worker.

Instead of answering him, Sofia turned her head to the side, sliding her lips over his. She moaned into that kiss as his hands dipped lower into her top, slipping under her bra and relishing the skin of her breasts underneath.

Desire roared to life inside of him, and a part of him urged himself towards caution. They were no longer in the privacy of his home, and they couldn't act with impunity—not without risking both of their professional reputations. Sofia was at far greater risk than him for that. He would be on his way in a couple of weeks' time, and she'd be left to clean up the mess they'd both willingly created.

But something about her touch, about the small mewls coming from her closed lips as his tongue clashed with hers, completely enthralled him and almost robbed him of any sense. Almost.

With an amount of self-restraint he didn't realise he was capable of, Carlos stopped kissing her. Sofia let out a huff of surprise when he straightened up, pulling his hands away from her and taking a step back.

'I ran away with myself,' he said when he read the silent question of what had just happened in her eyes. 'We're both new to rule-breaking, so I think we should start small. For example, if we are keen on breaking some more fraternisation rules, why don't we do it where people can't walk in on us?'

Sofia's eyes rounded, and her gaze darted about

as if to double-check that no one had been in the room with them when their exchange had started.

His timing couldn't have been more on point, for they both heard the persistent squeak of rubber shoes against the hospital floor that was getting louder by the second—until a woman stepped into the staff room, one hand holding a tablet while the other rested on top of her pregnant belly.

'Bella! I thought Sebastián said you were off today?' Sofia jumped to her feet, the chair she sat on skittering over the floor with a loud screech— as if it had picked up on the nervous energy alive in the room. She was clearly aware of how close they had got to being caught in their heated embrace.

Something that didn't pass by Isabella either. She narrowed her eyes and looked between them. 'He certainly wants me to take more time off, but I'm not stopping work until these babies are ready to pop out.'

A frown appeared on Sofia's lips. 'You are carrying around triplets. That's a high-risk pregnancy, and you definitely shouldn't be working until they are "ready to pop out".' She raised her fingers to mimic air quotes as she repeated the other woman's words.

'You sound like Seb,' Bella said with an eye-roll. 'And don't try to change the subject. What are *you* two doing here?'

Before Carlos could say anything, Sofia opened her mouth. 'W-we were…' Her voice trailed off as her eyes darted around, looking for an excuse. 'We were going over some patient notes for a surgery we did earlier this week.'

Bella levelled a stare at her that said she saw through the lie—which wasn't all that difficult. Though Sofia had many talents, he realised lying wasn't one of them.

For the second time in a short span, their luck pulled through when both their pagers began sounding at the same time.

'An emergency surgery just came in,' he said to Sofia, then nodded at Isabella before squeezing past her and down the corridor to the operating rooms, with Sofia's steps echoing behind as she followed him.

The heat of their moment in the staff room still clung to her cheeks when Sofia finished scrubbing and stepped into the OR. They had washed in silence, but the tension between them remained in place as neither of them acknowledged what had happened—both between them and with Isabella.

What was strange was that her heart was racing from being caught, but it wasn't fear that had her pulse elevated. No, she had Carlos to thank for that. Though they had spent several hours together the other day, she hadn't expected him to be so forward at work. Not when they were both normally focused on their careers and professional reputations.

In her mind, Sofia knew she should be horrified that one of the senior leaders of the hospital had almost caught her in an inappropriate position with a colleague. She had given up so much to get to this point in her career. Her dedication to her job had been the reason why her relationships had never worked out—including Daniel, who had chosen to punish her for her priorities in the cruellest way.

But there was nothing but excitement dancing in the pit of her stomach. Carlos's touch sent lightning through her body, filling her with a longing unlike anything she'd ever felt. The only regret she had about what they had done in the staff room was that their shift wasn't over yet.

'What are we working on?' Carlos asked as he stepped into the room. If he had any feelings about what had happened between them, he wasn't showing them.

'We have Manny Vargas, a thirty-five-year-old male involved in an accident on his bicycle. Bystanders reported to the paramedics that he was hit by a car and thrown several feet upon impact,' the junior doctor assisting them said, relaying the information from the ER.

Sofia noticed a small crease appearing between Carlos's brows, and she watched him closely as the junior surgeon informed them about the vitals of the patient and the results of the CT scans and X-rays they'd already performed.

The last time they had worked on a car crash victim, Carlos had suffered a panic attack. Since then she had watched him carefully whenever they were in any high-stress situation, noting any differences in his behaviour as they worked. She hadn't seen anything since and wasn't sure that there was anything now, either.

'So we need to have a look at the ruptured spleen and the fracture in his femur,' Carlos said, then glanced at her. 'You run the surgery on the spleen. I'll examine at the leg.'

'Right.' Sofia nodded, pushing the worry about him to the back of her mind. Splitting up surgical responsibilities was one of the techniques Carlos had been teaching everyone—including her. Even though his self-assured air still grated on her, she had to admit that he'd brought everyone on the surgical team to a different level with his teachings.

She stepped up to the patient. The surgical field was already prepped and ready to go. 'Can you bring up the CT scans for me?' Yasmine, the trainee surgeon next to her, nodded, then walked over to the computer and brought up the pictures. That there was damage in that area was obvious the second the scans loaded. The active haemorrhage from the blood pooling around the spleen and other organs stood out in a brighter colour, giving Sofia an idea about the severity of the case.

'There will be internal bleeding, so let's get the sponges ready to soak it all up. Chances are we'll have to remove the spleen if the damage is too severe.' There usually was no other option, and though every surgery was invasive, this was a better outcome than having to remove a kidney or a part of the liver. With high-impact accidents like that, they never knew where the damage would lie.

She received the scalpel from the OR assistant, then opened an incision in the left upper quadrant of the patient's abdomen to expose the way to the spleen. Once she was there, she worked with Yasmine to mobilise the spleen by detaching it from other organs so she could assess it and make her choice about the next steps. 'Put some more sponges in here,' she instructed when blood began pooling in the abdominal cavity again.

Every so often, Sofia glanced over at Carlos, who stood further down the patient at his exposed leg, working with another junior doctor. From the snippets of conversation floating over to her, she could tell they were attempting to set the bone, but the fracture was looking more complex than they'd initially thought. Carlos would ask for help if he needed it, wouldn't he? She didn't know what high-stress situations were triggers for him, and all she had to go by were traffic accidents.

Why had they not spoken about this again? That had been the reason she'd tried to catch up with him in the hospital last week, only for Carlos to dodge her. Then, when she finally had found him again coincidentally, he'd not been wearing a shirt, and all the attraction simmering beneath the surface had just bubbled forward.

Under the bright light of the OR, she could see a film of sweat on his brow, though she knew her own was looking similar. To keep everyone involved safe, they had to wear several layers of protection, and it could get hot in the operating room, especially if you had to set bones, which took a lot more force. Though if they had to move around a lot, they'd wait until the spleen was out.

Sofia pushed those thoughts away. They would have to talk about it after. It was no use if she worried throughout surgeries they did together if he was in distress. They needed to come up with a safe way of dealing with it—like many other surgeons suffering from PTSD had.

'Okay, now that it's secured, we will ligate the spleen and then remove it.' She handed the tool to Yasmine, who took it with an eager nod and stepped closer to the patient. Sofia watched and instructed the junior surgeon as she ligated the smaller arteries and veins before coming to the big one. She paused, adjusting her grip, then went to work while Sofia kept suctioning to keep the surgical area clear.

'We have to wait until we put in the screws.' Carlos's voice drifted to her ear, and she looked up just as he moved closer to her, his eyes narrowing slightly in a smile she couldn't see underneath his surgical mask.

'How is the break looking?' she asked him, her eyes back on the patient.

'Complex, but we can place a rod and screws right now to set the bone, and hopefully we won't need a second surgery.' From the corner of her eye, she could tell his expression was serious. 'He is facing a long road towards recovery, that's for sure.'

Sofia followed the hand of the junior surgeon as she went on to ligate the main artery of the spleen—a task that required the utmost delicacy as it represented the main blood flow.

'Anything we can do to assist?' Carlos asked, and she shook her head.

'We're about ready to remove the spleen. Once that's done, we'll close back up, and you guys can get on drilling away.' She paused, looking over at the leg that was still open but covered with a surgical sheet to keep it secured. 'It must be a complex fracture if you need to set it with a rod. Do we need to page someone from orthopaedics?'

Carlos shook his head. 'I've spent almost a year working with a guy in São Paulo who was the head of the orthopaedics department. His wife runs the hospital they worked at and wanted to free up more of his time to do volunteer work, so they asked me to come in and optimise their processes. Learned a lot about orthopaedic surgery in the process.'

Sofia's eyebrows rose at that piece of information. 'I didn't know that about you.'

'There are probably a lot of things you don't know about me.' The chuckle that underpinned his response was gentle, meant to tease her more than anything else. But it struck at a place of insecurity inside her chest. She really didn't know all that much about him—other than she simply couldn't resist him.

Whenever they spoke, they would mostly have clashing professional opinions, or argue about some triviality in the hospital. Those arguments stopped when they stepped into the OR, where they became one team with one mind as they worked on saving the patients under their care.

She had shared some things about her past, but he hadn't. Not only that, but he had made it a point to mention that he *wouldn't* share anything personal. So the disappointment pooling in the pit of her stomach was out of place.

Would he even tell her what triggered his panic attacks? Sofia had spoken about herself, had even shared with him that she hadn't ever had a casual affair. He'd listened to her and taken the time to understand where her nervous energy had come from so he could find a solution for it. Wasn't it strange that she didn't know anything about his past or what had brought him here?

'All the blood supplies are cut off. We are ready to remove the spleen,' Yasmine said, and Sofia handed over the aspirator as she looked around the surgical field.

'Good job,' she said with a smile, then began across the patient but paused when Carlos held out a plastic bag. She took it from him and fitted it over the spleen, then nodded to the junior surgeon to start cutting.

Her eyes flittered back toward Carlos, who was observing the surgery without making a sound or even moving his face. Nothing about the situation was unusual or should make her feel as nervous as she did. Yet her nerves were frayed, and she wondered not for the first time what she'd got herself into. This whole affair was so far away from 'playing it safe' that she couldn't even see the boundaries. And even though she knew that,

Sofia didn't want to quit. With all her failed relationships, this one somehow felt for the first
time like she was in control—like Carlos knew
exactly what she needed from a man.

She just couldn't get emotionally invested in
him. He was leaving Buenos Aires in less than
two weeks. They had agreed this was just for
fun. Instead of thinking that Carlos was the one
she needed, Sofia had to remind herself that what
Carlos had *shown* her was what she needed. It had
nothing to do with him personally.

There was something oddly calming about post-
surgery silence. After they removed the spleen,
they had finished up setting the screws and the
rod for the broken leg, then checked for other
sources of bleeding before closing the patient up.
Any follow-up surgeries would be handled by the
specialists. A flurry of motion filled the OR as
they prepped for patient transport. Then the team
exited—leaving the senior surgeons behind as
they were having a quiet conversation.

The second the door closed and cut them off
from the outside world, something in Carlos's
face changed. As if he was dropping some mask
he forced himself to keep on in front of junior
staff.

'This was a bad break. I can't even imagine
what the accident must have been like,' Carlos

said as they walked over to the bin to throw away their surgical gowns. Then they entered the scrub room, each of them stepping to a sink and quickly washing potential contamination off their hands and arms.

'All things considered, Manny pulled through. If the broken leg doesn't need any more surgery, then I think he's lucky to just lose his spleen. Orthopaedics will have to see if he needs anything else after some physical therapy,' Sofia replied.

She gave him a sidelong glance, her eyes narrowing as she tried to unravel his expression. The calm exterior he usually projected showed some fine lines—as if the pressure on him was increasing. Was she right to think that traffic accidents bothered him? Had something happened in his past—maybe a bad surgery—that he carried around with him?

Shutting off the water, Sofia turned sideways to face him. She hardly knew anything about Carlos, and even though he'd warned her he didn't do personal questions, she resolved to ask some, anyway. They had already established the casual nature of their affair. What harm could a few questions do?

'You're originally from Brazil, right?' she asked, earning herself a raised eyebrow from him.

'Did you…read my biography somewhere?' His lips twitched in an amused smile that smoothed away the lines of worry. Sofia's heart squeezed at the sight. That was a good reaction to what might be considered a personal question.

'Just curious about what made you leave your country. My whole family is here in the city, and even though I don't see them often because I'm usually too busy working, I can rely on them the same way they know they can rely on me.'

Something intangible fluttered over his expression as she mentioned her family. A myriad of emotions, as if he wasn't sure what to think or feel. When it settled down, she could see a faint curiosity in his eyes.

'I take it none of them are doctors?' he asked, and Sofia shook her head.

'No, so of course they are very proud of me. I'm the only one in my family, which means any larger family gathering just turns into clinic hours.' Though she liked to complain about it, it didn't bother her all that much. Because she had dedicated her adult life to her career, her parents and her brother had been the only ones to stick it out with her. They didn't complain when they didn't see her for weeks on end because they understood how important this was to her. It was this kind of understanding and patience she thought she had found with Daniel, only to be proved wrong.

'What do they do?' The spark of curiosity in

his eyes turned brighter, like he was enjoying himself a bit more than a minute ago. Another hopeful sign that she maybe could also learn a bit more about him.

'They run a horticultural farm mostly focused on local demands. They attend the farmer's markets in their area and sell to smaller *minimercados*,' she said, the fond memories she had of the tiny grocery stores in her old neighbourhood making her smile.

'And your parents run the entire operation by themselves?' he asked, and raised his eyebrows when she nodded.

'Them and my older brother and his wife. They live on the land they cultivate—about an hour's drive from here. Another reason why I don't get to visit often. Their schedules are just as hectic as mine since they grow different vegetables and fruits all throughout the year.'

A stab of guilt poked at her, a familiar sensation at this point. She knew she should make more time for her family, but with her career being in the place it was, she had to put everything into it if she wanted to claim the success she was dreaming of. At least her family understood that she had to give up other things to achieve what she'd set out to do.

Carlos stepped closer, putting a hand on her

upper arm and giving it an affectionate squeeze. 'That sounds like a hard life for them.'

'It is,' Sofia said with a nod. 'That's why the thought of leaving Buenos Aires has never crossed my mind. When things are tight, I help them out. Like when they need new equipment, or when they can't afford to repair one of the cars. They supported me throughout med school, and now it's on me to give back.'

He stood close enough that she had to tilt her head back to look up at him. The touch of something ethereal had returned in his gaze, an intangible sensation that skipped the short distance between them and crawled down her spine. 'They're lucky to have you,' he murmured.

'You don't have anyone waiting for you back in Brazil?' she asked cautiously.

'No,' he said. Then his hand came up to her face, cupping her cheek.

'No? No family or friends waiting to hear about your adventures abroad?' How could this man be all alone? Sure, they had clashed during their initial meetings—they still did, their attraction to each other not having changed that. But, despite his sometimes abrasive nature, Carlos was inherently a kind man.

His thumb traced the curve of her cheekbone, sweeping up and down. Its arc slowed ever so slightly when he said, 'No one.'

There was a tremor in his voice. It was faint, barely there and easily missed if they weren't standing so close together, their breaths mingling. Then, before she could ask the next question building in her mind, Carlos bent down and slid his mouth over hers—and like the times before, she melted against him with a sigh.

His tongue darted over her lips, begging for entry, and she more than willingly yielded. With one simple touch, he had her on edge again already, forgetting who she was and what they had been talking about just a minute ago.

Dear God, how was this man so intoxicating? There was nothing in her life she could compare this connection to because they all faded away in comparison. Carlos was like a warm breeze passing through her, leaving her more energised each time he touched her—and also leaving behind a strange sense of emptiness whenever he left.

Control was slipping out of her grasp as Carlos's lips left hers, trailing down her neck. 'Will you have drinks with me tonight?' he whispered against her skin, the gravel in his voice drawing her attention.

'That depends… Did you go shopping?' Their no-strings-attached agreement was about sex, and even though a part of her wanted to have drinks with him simply to enjoy his company, her guarded heart demanded she enforce the boundaries they had set. There had to be a purpose behind their meetings or they would risk getting too close. The lines were already blurring, their attraction burning so fiercely that they couldn't keep their hands off each other at work.

His chuckle rumbled through the room, enveloping her with tendrils of gentle warmth. 'I did.'

'Good. It would have been a bit awkward if we had to explain to the pharmacist here why two trauma surgeons needed some condoms,' she replied, then took a step backwards, peeling herself out of his arms. 'You have a place in mind?'

'I do.' His eyes raked over her, tempting her to step closer again. But something about him caught her attention.

'You're a hard person to get to know, Carlos,' she said, sliding further away from him when he tilted his head, confusion blooming on his face. Throughout this conversation, he hadn't really answered a single thing about himself but had somehow got her to talk about her family.

But why would her words confuse him if his secrecy was by design?

Neither of them got to say anything to follow up her statement. The doors swung open and one of the junior doctors stepped in, freezing in his steps when he noticed two of his superiors just standing in the room looking at each other.

Sofia took that as her queue to leave and made

a mental note to no longer get caught up with Carlos when they were at the hospital. This was the second time today that someone had almost walked in on them.

'I'll see you later, Dr Cabrera. Just text me the details,' she said, then squeezed past the other person to leave the scrub room.

CHAPTER EIGHT

YOU'RE A HARD person to get to know, Carlos.

The words wove themselves through his consciousness throughout the rest of the day, popping back up in between seeing patients in the ICU and taking care of some consultations in the ER. Carlos didn't understand what exactly was bringing his attention back to Sofia's statement, but something was, and the more he rolled it around in his head, the less he understood.

It had sounded like an accusation, and the strange thing was that he could understand that—despite him saying that he wouldn't answer any questions about himself. A few days ago, that had seemed like a reasonable boundary, but he could understand what it looked like from Sofia's standpoint. She had learned nothing about him through many of their conversations, while he treasured the morsels of knowledge he had gathered from her.

Carlos wasn't sure he knew how to do casual, and his need to know more about her showed that.

Yet when she had turned the questions around to him, the walls had pressed in on him, and he'd shut down, not letting her see anything on the surface and definitely nothing further below.

He would be lying if he said that he hadn't enjoyed hearing about the farm her parents ran. When she had shared that with him, a thousand more questions had popped up in his head, and he'd shoved them all down.

But then she had asked who was waiting for him in Brazil, and it had taken everything in him not to close down instantly. The defence mechanism inside of him relating to anything connected to Rosa was strong and easily triggered without people even knowing it. That was the reason why he kept people at arm's length since becoming a widower.

How would these people react if they knew he'd been the one responsible for the accident that had killed his wife? Neither the police nor the insurance company could find any fault in his behaviour, but Carlos knew better. He had promised to protect Rosa for the rest of her life on the day of their wedding. He had failed at that, and now she was gone.

With a sigh, Carlos reached for his drink and took a sip before setting it down on the bar again, his eyes flittering to the entrance before looking at the clock on his phone. If he knew anything about Sofia and her preference for rules, she would walk through those doors the moment the minute ticked over to when they had agreed to meet.

He kept his eyes on the phone, staring at the number until it finally moved. Then he looked up. Not a heartbeat later, Sofia walked through the doors. His jaw tightened—along with something further down—when he watched her approach him. The black dress she'd chosen hugged every single curve with such perfection that he had to assume someone had made this dress specifically for her. The neckline dipped down, accentuating the slight swell of her breasts. The skirt of the dress fell down to her feet, but a slit almost all the way up to the top of her hip revealed her thigh with every other step.

She was a vision of femininity, walking towards him as if there were clouds under her feet—almost floating. Effortless.

Her appearance had him staring at her in stunned silence until she came to a stop in front of him, a small smile curling her lips.

'Is this seat taken?' she asked, and the blush glowing beneath her skin told him how much effort she had put into this line—that she was trying to flirt with him.

He stood up, laying his hand on her hip and savouring the feel of the silky fabric underneath his fingertips. His eyes dipped down to her neckline of their own accord, and only when Sofia chuckled did he look back up.

'None of the words in my mind are anywhere near appropriate to say,' he told her with a smirk, and male satisfaction rushed through his veins when the blush on her cheeks intensified.

'Is that a line you found works particularly well with women?' she asked tartly as she took her seat next to his.

'I wouldn't know. You're the first one to hear these words.' Something about the way she raised her eyebrows at him with widened eyes bothered him, though he couldn't quite pin it down. It was the same look she had given him when he'd told her he didn't have any protection with him. Like that idea was somehow ridiculous, because how could he possibly not?

He shook off the thought when the bartender stepped up to the bar. 'What can I get you?'

'Oh.' Sofia looked at Carlos's glass, then let her gaze run along the shelves before stopping at a bottle he couldn't see. 'Could you make me a Clarito?'

The bartender smiled with a nod, then went on to pour gin, vermouth, and some orange bitters into a glass. The clinking of ice mixed with the fast-paced music and the fragments of conversation from other patrons. It was that perfect backdrop of sound that had Carlos coming back here often enough. With so much going on around him, it was easy to let go and just follow his strands of thoughts wherever they might lead him. Even though he wasn't much of a drinker, this space had become a safe haven for him in Buenos Aires.

And now he was staring at Sofia, who he had willingly invited into this space.

'What's a Clarito?' he asked, and followed her gaze to watch as the bartender put a martini glass on the counter and began pouring the liquid into it. When he was happy with how the twist of lemon zest sat inside the glass, he pushed it over to Sofia.

'It's a popular cocktail around here, and one of the few drinks I like,' she said, then raised her glass at him.

Carlos obliged with a smile, clinking their glasses together and then taking a sip of his own drink. 'Don't drink much?'

She shook her head as she put the glass down. 'When would I ever have time to go out? Especially now, with you stealing all my surgeries if I'm not careful.'

'I believe I explained myself about that *and* took appropriate steps to remedy it. I'm hardly in surgery any more.' He leaned into the joke she had started, mounting his mock defence.

Sofia laughed, and something inside his chest loosened at that sound. A soothing warmth bloomed, sending soft shivers down his body. 'Yes, but you replaced surgery with following me around to find opportunities to make out with me. I'm not sure that's more appropriate.'

The smile tugging on his lips was one suffused with the energy he'd been battling all day whenever he'd seen her around the hospital. She wasn't wrong about his intentions for her. But he still shrugged as he said, 'I can stop if you want.'

'No!' The word came from her lips way too fast. As she, too, realised this, the blush that bloomed on her cheeks was exquisite. Carlos almost had to bite his fist to keep himself from hauling her into his arms.

'Eh… I mean… I don't *want* you to stop, but—'

This time, he couldn't hold himself back. He got off the barstool and stepped into the V of her legs, forcing her to look up at him. 'Good. Not touching you costs me more willpower than I can muster. You're all I've been thinking about.'

Carlos observed her throat flutter as she swallowed, her uneven breaths skittering across his face. 'I still don't think it's smart to do these things in the hospital,' she said hoarsely, and he nodded.

'I agree. Not the best look were we to get caught, and I don't want to leave you alone with the fallout when I end up leaving.' Though kissing her had been the highlight of his day at work, filling him with a spark he hadn't sensed inside of him in many years. Work had become his ultimate distraction in life, letting him forget about the things weighing him down. Now he was excited again, and not just to see Sofia and do all the things he dreamt of doing to her. He also appreciated the challenge she brought to each case they worked together, the stubbornness and willingness to fight for what she believed was the right approach. She was drop-dead gorgeous, and she also wasn't afraid to clash with him and draw the best out of him as a result.

'It's been hard not being all over you today,' Carlos said, his hand coming to rest on her thigh.

Sofia smiled at that. 'Well… You kind of were.'

He blinked at her in surprise. Then his smile broadened into a grin as she reinforced the thoughts he'd just had without even knowing about them.

'It's not often I meet someone who is so eager to fight me every step of the way. Whenever I go to a new hospital, there are always people who dislike the change, but they usually get in line when their chief of surgery tells them to. Not you, though.' Affection exploded in the pit of his stomach when he said the last words.

Her face glowed. He wasn't sure if it was due

to what he said or because of how close his thumb was to her inner thigh. 'I'm not challenging you because I dislike change. The things you taught everyone are important and good improvements to our overall service quality. You just don't have to be such a jerk about it.'

Her eyes widened, as if she hadn't meant to say that and it had just slipped out. 'What I meant—' she began, but then a laugh burst out of his mouth, deep and jovial.

'I get it. Our first few meetings weren't exactly smooth sailing, and I may have been harder on you that I needed to be.' He remembered the steel in his voice when he had clashed with her in the OR. That much hadn't changed about them, though now he realised their tension might have come from this unexpected place he found himself in with her.

'Who knew this is what was hiding underneath the gruff exterior?' She looked up at him teasingly through her lashes, her golden-flecked brown eyes filled with a twinkle that shot straight through him. This wasn't a tone he was used to from her.

'Are you flirting with me?' he asked, the smile on his lips growing when her eyes widened.

'You can see what I mean now when I said I've never done anything casual. I can't even be subtle about my flirting attempts.' She reached for her glass, taking a sip. When she put it back down, Carlos leaned in and brushed a kiss onto her lips, tasting the leftover Clarito on them.

'We don't have to do anything you don't want, you know?' he said, even though his stomach sank at the thought that they could part ways like this.

The speed with which Sofia shook her head put him at ease. 'I definitely want to be here. It's just that…' She paused, mulling over her words. 'It may sound stupid, but I put so much effort into my career and being the best at it that "being the best" became my standard. So if I'm in situations that are outside of my expertise or don't follow a path I can read up on, then I become hesitant.'

Carlos couldn't help but smile. The hyper-competitiveness of surgeons in general was a reason why it was sometimes much harder for him to teach them. Trying new things led to errors, and they were taught to avoid mistakes or lives could be lost. 'Going outside your comfort zone is the only way to push yourself towards being "the best." Consider this an opportunity to do that,' he said. When the beats of a familiar song hit his ear, an idea struck him.

'Do you know how to dance?' As he asked the question, some patrons sitting at the tables of the bar got to their feet.

A line appeared between Sofia's brows. 'Dance? Like what? Samba?'

'Yes, or more specifically—tango. It's the dance of your people.'

'Maybe as a child, but I don't remember any of it...' There was a hesitation after her words, like she wanted to ask why, but she already knew.

Carlos grinned at that. 'Well, then consider this another way to challenge your comfort zone,' he said, before pulling her up on her feet and leading her to where other patrons were already swaying together.

Of course Carlos knew how to dance. Because apparently there wasn't a single thing on this planet this man didn't excel at. She saw the challenge in his eyes as he grabbed her hand while placing his other one on the small of her back, drawing her closer until their breaths mingled.

'Listen to the music, feel the rhythm of my body and let me guide you,' he said as he looked down at her, the mischievous spark in his eyes only steeling her resolve. She might not know a single thing about tango, but she knew how to approach a challenge.

The first few steps were stiff, wound tight by the concentration she put into every move, trying her best to mirror what Carlos was showing her. His own steps were smooth, flowing from one position to the next while continuing his guidance with soft brushes of his hand against her back or his thigh against hers.

His fluidity didn't surprise her, not after what she'd observed at the capoeira gym. Anticipation for this evening had been slowly building inside of her, but with him close to her now—their movements and glances intimate—it had reached a fever pitch. She couldn't remember the last time she had felt this way, need and desire so tightly coiled in her chest that all she could focus on was where his body connected with hers.

The music flowed through the air, caressing her ear and moving along her body in smooth and sensual beats, and each step became easier to follow until Carlos was swinging her around, his guidance keeping her moving along with him.

'Capoeira and tango. How did you get into dancing?' she asked when she felt confident enough in their rhythm to let some of her focus go into a conversation.

'Capoeira was big in the neighbourhood I grew up in. Every afternoon when I'd get back from school, there would be music filling the streets as people grabbed their drums and guitars to join the *roda*—the circle of people, if you remember.'

Sofia nodded, the memory feeling so far away already. Their attraction to each other really had been brewing underneath the surface if it had boiled over so fast after they'd admitted to it. 'People would just stand in circles on the street and fight each other?'

The chuckle coming from Carlos shot down her spine and settled in an aching pinch in the pit of her stomach. 'We don't fight. The art of capoeira is *avoiding* any direct hits. Sure, we use kicks and punches, but they're meant to form a game, challenging your partner into quick thinking and flexibility,' he explained as he pulled her closer to him. 'It's way more a dance than a fight.'

Sofia's skin heated when his voice dropped low. 'I didn't even know it existed, or that there was a whole gym dedicated to it.'

'You never seen them performing it at Carnival?' he asked, and raised his eyebrows when she shook her head.

'Carnival is prime time for injuries and accidents, so the most I get to enjoy Carnival is when colourful costumed people come into the OR with light injuries.' Her longest shifts usually happened around that time, as the city let loose for a few days. 'Wait, does that mean you're performing next weekend?'

A smile appeared on her lips when he nodded. 'My contract is wrapping up just before Carnival starts, so I should be able to enjoy it.'

His contract? Even though his eventual departure from Hospital General de Buenos Aires had been one of the primary motivators for her to agree to this affair, she didn't realise she'd been ignoring how close he actually was to leaving. Was there enough time to finally pierce through his shell? Was there even a reason to do it? He had rebuffed any of her attempts to ask even simple questions about his private life. Someone less stubborn than her would take the hint and leave it be. But Sofia hadn't got to where she was now by *not* persisting when things got difficult. Maybe it was all about how she asked him the questions.

'And tango? Did capoeira teach you that you like dancing?'

Carlos hesitated. His step didn't falter, and they were still moving with the beat of the music, his attentive guidance never stopping. But she could see that behind his eyes, where a fire was still burning, there was now a flutter. He was making a decision, only she couldn't even guess what it was. There were much more probing questions clinging to her lips, yet somehow she had uncovered something deep with the question about tango.

He looked at her, the flame in those dark eyes flickering. Then he raised his gaze to look at a point behind her. His throat worked, and then he said, 'My late wife enjoyed dancing.'

The music faded away, and it took Sofia a moment to notice the songs were changing—because the piece of information he'd just dropped in front of her had all her senses occupied. She stared at him wide-eyed. Then her attention was caught by the dancers around them. Some of them were shuffling away as the tempo of the new song was slower. Others pulled each other close, and gentle whispers filled the air with a strange sense of intimacy.

'Oh, Carlos… I'm so—' He shook his head, interrupting her, and when he looked back down, there was a smile on his face. A less bright version of the one she'd seen on him just a few moments ago. But she understood what he was trying to tell her. He'd wanted her to have this information about him—wanted to forge that connection despite his initial insistence that he wouldn't. But he was not open to talking about it any more than he already had.

His arms tightened around her waist, pulling her closer as they swayed to the slow beat of a bossa nova song, and Sofia rested her head on his chest—feeling close to him in this moment. She should not feel as elated about him sharing something personal about him as she was right now. That wasn't part of the plan, and it didn't fit into the rules they had established around their fling. This was supposed to be physical in nature only. But after trying for so long, she'd finally found a way past his walls. How could she step back from him when he had let her in?

'It was some time ago now. I wanted you to know that the womanising version of me you have in your head doesn't actually exist. I haven't...' He stopped himself, and Sofia leaned in more when his flat palms caressed up and down her back. 'What I mean to say is—this is special to me.'

Sofia's heart beat so fast, she was sure if she opened her mouth it would leap right out. Was that his way of saying he didn't usually do casual, either? Or was it that he didn't want this to be *just* casual sex? The meaning of Carlos suddenly opening up to her wasn't clear to her, but the words to ask the important question wouldn't form in her head. This was again a place unfamiliar to her.

His hands reached the top of her back, his fingers grazing over the exposed skin there and leaving a trail of small fires in their wake.

'Does your offer to show me some capoeira moves still stand?' she asked, letting the things he had shared with her sit between them in companionable silence. She didn't know how to talk about it or what to say, but she knew she didn't want to let their personal connection that went beyond the physical disappear just yet. And the first thing popping into her mind when thinking about the things Carlos cared about was capoeira.

His fingers stalled for a fraction of a second before they resumed their caress. 'Sure, but you won't be able to move in this dress. How about we continue this at my place?'

CHAPTER NINE

CARLOS WAITED FOR about a second between stepping out of the elevator and into the penthouse with Sofia and hauling her into his arms, into a deep kiss. The struggle to keep his hands off her all day had been so much more exhausting than he could have imagined. He was drawn to her whenever he saw her, and no matter how much he sated his hunger with her, it kept coming back with an unreal fierceness.

It was all because of this moment that had been in the making for a while. That was what he told himself as his tongue delved into her mouth, meeting her eagerness stroke for stroke. There was something intangible, inexplicable to his burning desire. After such a long absence from his life, the resurgence of it took Carlos aback, and he didn't know what to make of it. If someone had asked him just last month if he had any interest in being with a woman, his answer would have been no. His job was all he cared about, his career what he poured all of his attention into.

Then Sofia had entered his life like the whirl-wind she was. Her challenges to his work had thrown him off guard, leaving a tiny gap for her to nestle into. Now she was in his brain, had taken up residence there as if he hadn't guarded him-self from such intrusions for the last five years. What threw him off even more than her having got as close to him as she had was his comfort amidst all of it. In his mind he knew he should retreat, that he shouldn't have brought her here in the first place.

He had told her about Rosa. Even tiny morsels of information about his late wife remained under lock and key from everyone, and he wasn't sure what had happened there. It didn't slip out. No, when she'd asked that question, he had reached for his basket of excuses, coming up with one ex-planation or another why he knew how to dance tango. But something inside of him had insisted on telling her the truth, on giving her this one piece of information in return for all the things she had already shared about herself. For the role she had played in his healing journey—whether she knew it or not.

'Is this how you start your lessons with every-one?' Sofia huffed between heated kisses, draw-ing a chuckle from him.

'No, this is just for you,' he replied, and sensed in the depth of his chest how much he meant exactly those words. This was not just for her—it was *only* for her. In a life he had designed to be fleeting, she had found a way to make herself far more permanent than anyone else he'd met.

Her lips were swollen already, her breath coming out quickly and sliding over his skin in the sensual promise of what tonight would be.

'What makes me so special to deserve all of your attention?' She tried to hide the edge in her tone, but Carlos picked up on it. He gripped her hips and held her away from him so he could look at her.

'Whoever didn't make you feel special in the past was a fool, Sofia,' he said, delighting as her lips fell open a bit more. 'For the last few weeks, you have been challenging me at every turn, forcing me to up my game and refine my methods.'

He paused as more information about himself threatened to spill out of his mouth. Her words echoed in his mind. He *was* a hard man to get to know, and he had done that on purpose. What if people learned too much about him? What if they realised he was a highly regarded trauma surgeon who found it incredibly traumatic to treat patients involved in a car accident? His reputation was on the line.

But Sofia hadn't hesitated—and she had kept his confidence without him having to ask. She had discovered this one thing about him by mistake. Whatever else she'd learned about him, Carlos wanted it to come from him.

'You saw me at my worst when everyone only knows me as this fixer—coming into hospitals and upping everyone's game. It's disruptive, but in the end everyone walks away better. Stronger. Some would have doubted my abilities after seeing me like that.' Though their conversation grew serious, Carlos didn't let her forget the purpose of her visit to his flat. While he spoke, he traced his hands up and down her sides, brushing over the exposed skin of her arms and raising the hair along them.

Sofia's eyes fluttered closed for a few breaths. When she opened them again, fire lit them, and Carlos's knees almost gave out from underneath him.

'I understand what this line of work can do to you,' was all she said to his confession, and somehow Carlos knew that simple acknowledgement to be enough.

Because if any other doctor had told him that specific surgeries or situations triggered a stress response, he knew he wouldn't think less of them but rather work on whatever had brought it forth.

But his case was different. He was directly responsible for Rosa's death. No matter who else was on the road that night, he had been behind the wheel.

Carlos pushed those thoughts away, willing himself to stay present in the moment. Negotiating his complex feelings around past mistakes was his daily struggle, but it eased when he could distract himself. Work had served him as a faithful diversion, but Sofia... She was something else entirely.

His hands paused on her hips, and he grabbed her, spinning her around so she was with her front against the wall. 'You always want to have your feet grounded before you perform any move,' he said as he squatted down to slide her feet out of her shoes.

When he came back up, his hands slid underneath her dress, caressing her naked skin. 'You want to be as unrestricted as possible,' he continued as he found the zipper of her dress, pulling it down and peeling her dress away.

His mouth went dry. She was naked underneath.

'Unrestricted?' she asked, turning around with a lazy smile that almost brought him to his knees.

Her hand came to rest on his chest. As she traced over him, she undid every button of his shirt until it hung open. He wasn't sure whether he had picked up hesitation or inexperience from her last time. Something had had her tense and unable to let go until they had talked through it.

None of that was present today. No, she looked

at him with the sensual smile of a siren, luring him in with the song of her swaying hips as she took a step backwards.

Carlos shrugged off his shirt, then grabbed Sofia with hungry hands, his mouth coming down on hers as he pushed her against the wall. She writhed against him, her legs circling around him and pressing against his erection. The groan loosened from his throat came from an ancient place that he hadn't accessed or even looked at in the last five years.

He wrapped his arms around her waist as he pushed off the wall, carrying her to the bedroom. Sofia let out a yelp when he deposited her on the bed, the sound driving through him like a hot spear.

Carlos kicked off his shoes and hissed when he felt Sofia's hands pull at his waistband, unbuttoning his trousers and pushing them down his legs—along with his underwear. Where they had moved at a leisurely pace last time, today was dictated by urgency, their need running too hot to leave room for delicacy or patience.

Stepping out of his trousers, he turned around and grabbed a condom from the pack he'd bought last night after Sofia had left, safely stashed away in his nightstand. His hand trembled as he rolled it down his shaft—from need as much as from nerves.

Being with Sofia—getting to feel her all around him—had been an obsession in his mind ever since the fantasy had become a real possibility. Once he crossed this boundary, he'd never be able to go back again. The importance of this moment thundered through him, mingling with the need she kindled in him.

'You okay?' she asked, propped up on her elbows and looking at him.

His eyes raked over her, taking in every dip, every curve of her body. Her dark nipples were peaked, her breasts rising and falling with her rapid breathing, and he could already see the anticipation between her legs. But what caught his attention this time was how her hair fanned out behind her in a thick curtain of different shades of dark all mixing.

'I don't think I've ever seen you with your hair down,' he said gruffly, and her eyes widened.

The air between them grew intimate, the spark bouncing back and forth between them as Carlos put one knee on the bed and pushed forward. Sofia moaned when his weight settled between her thighs.

A tremble shook Carlos's body. 'You test my restraint, Sofia,' he rasped against the skin between her breasts.

'You showed supreme restraint last time. Do

we really need to exercise it again today?' Her mind was filled with the need for Carlos, and nothing else had space in it. What had happened between them in the bar was gone, their conversations trivial in comparison to the desire rising within her. This moment had been in the making for so long... To feel him now teasing her right where she wanted him more than anything else was too much.

'I'm not a selfish lover, *corazón*.' He dipped his head low, sucked one of her nipples into his mouth, and swirled his tongue around it.

Her back left the bed as she bowed into his touch, a tremble shaking her muscles one by one.

'It's not selfish if I'm asking for it,' she replied in a voice barely above a whisper.

'Mmm...' His voice vibrated onto her skin as he nipped at her other breast. She wasn't sure if the sound was savouring or contemplative— and she didn't have any space in her brain left to think about that when the pressure of his manhood nudged against her entrance.

'You're right. Maybe I am a selfish lover, after all,' he said when he came back up to her face, their noses touching as he looked at her. 'You are such perfection that it's hard to choose where to touch when each spot is so enticing.'

Even though they were naked in each other's arms, and had even been intimate with each other, his words brought heat to her cheeks. No one had ever said anything that made her feel this desirable.

'Carlos...' His name was a plea on her lips. Urgency wound her core tight, and she raised her hips, pressing against where she could feel him.

Above her, Carlos hissed, but then—finally and, oh, so slowly—the pressure at her entrance increased as he sunk into her with a deep groan that rumbled through her. Her muscles tensed, her body adjusting around him until the initial discomfort blurred away into the pleasurable sensation of their bodies combined.

Carlos moved his hips, and she moved with him, never taking her eyes off him. Their breaths mingled, became one, as they got closer to the edge together. When he slipped his hand between them to caress her, the little fires smouldering underneath the surface accelerated into a wildfire across her entire body.

A moan tore from her lips as her hips twitched, her muscles contracting when she reached her climax. Carlos kept moving in her, his pleasure mounting with each shortened breath. A strangled sound left his throat, one that sounded like her name. Then he slid his mouth over hers, drawing her into a long kiss filled with the tension and release they had worked up and found together in this moment.

* * *

A warm sensation trickled down her back and roused Sofia from her sleep. Still groggy and half-veiled in slumber, she tried to focus and figure out what woke her—until the memories of the night came back to her.

Carlos ran his fingers up and down her spine, stopping at her shoulder blade now and then before resuming their lazy caress. She sighed when the sensation turned from surprising to pleasant, and she leaned into the gentle touch. A part of her wanted to drift back to sleep, but he might have woken her for a reason. Was it time to leave already?

'I'm sorry I woke you up. Go back to sleep, sweetheart,' he whispered before she could ask—once again anticipating her needs.

'But then I'll miss how good this feels,' she replied as another warm shower of pleasure trickled through her.

'Oh, yeah? You like this?' His voice came closer as he shifted on the bed, and then his breath danced over her skin as he leaned closer. His hand drifted up to her shoulder and his mouth followed, feathering light kisses onto her skin.

She moaned her agreement, her head sinking back into the pillow. Her toes curled at the gentle touch, prompting her muscles to tense in a short stretch before going limp in his arms.

Every stretch of skin he touched came alive under his fingers, as if he could direct liquid flame through her body at his pleasure. The connection was explosive, and Sofia caught herself fantasising more than once about what it would be like to let herself slide down into the feelings he evoked in her. Would it be such a bad thing? She knew they were short-term, but keeping her guard up at every interaction with him was becoming more challenging—his skill at climbing her walls as impressive as everything else about him.

'I was trying to make out your tattoo in the bar last night,' he said against her skin, and Sofia realised why the path of his fingers had felt so familiar. 'The strand of DNA was just visible whenever we spun around, but I had no idea it turned into…this.'

His hands trailed downwards again, sweeping over her lower back. Her tattoo began there. A system of roots, delicately woven together, narrowed into a tree trunk that swept up her spine. Where branches and leaves would normally sprout out were helixes of DNA winding together.

Sofia tensed at the mention of her tattoo—an involuntary reaction from her that revealed far more than she intended. And by the way his hand stopped instantly, she knew he had picked up on it, too.

'You want me to stop?' he asked, and her heart softened at the concern lacing his voice.

'No, it's not that. It's…' She hesitated when the words formed in her head, unsure if she should say them. The warmth of his body drifted towards her, his touch so reassuring that she couldn't remember why she even *wanted* to be guarded.

'My ex didn't like the tattoo. He thought I had ruined my skin by getting it, and… I don't know why, but it just stuck with me.' She tensed again, readying herself to hear more negative feedback about her tattoo. Had Daniel been right? Was it really that ugly?

Warm breath teased her skin as Carlos exhaled behind her. He was quiet for a few heartbeats. Then she gasped as his hand pressed into her lower back.

'The one you mentioned yesterday?' he asked, his fingers tracing each individual root at the base of her spine.

'What?' Sofia wasn't sure if she didn't understand the question or if his caresses had her in a daze.

'Last week, when we were talking about what we wanted, you said you didn't have any experience in casual relationships, and you mentioned Daniel. He said that to you about your tattoo?'

She nodded, fighting the discomfort rising inside her. The second her ex's name had left her lips, she had regretted it. Only for him to come up again. Would she ever be rid of his looming shadow? 'Yes, that was him.'

Behind her, Carlos kept the steady pace of his hand up and down her back, his touch calming while his silence ratcheted up the tension inside of her. He hadn't said if *he* liked the tattoo—not that it mattered. He would only be a fleeting presence in her life, and what she should do was to take the pleasure he offered her and just enjoy it for what it was.

The sheets rustled when Carlos pulled her closer, tangling their legs. 'What else has he done that still lingers with you?'

Sofia paused, both to consider and to soak up the warmth his touch brought her. Should she really talk about Daniel again? Sharing something like that didn't fit into her understanding of a casual relationship. It also violated their rule of no personal questions. A rule that they had already stepped on several times over.

'He…cheated on me. Found himself a new girlfriend while we were still together and posted about it on Instagram. A lot of my relationships failed because they weren't able to cope with my unpredictable schedule—which I can understand. But he was very understanding and so encouraging about my career. Never said a single thing about needing me to be with him more. Not until…' Sofia closed her eyes as the memories of their confrontation came back to her. She braced herself for the hurt they caused, for the nails digging into her heart. But none of those usual sensations came. 'I confronted him about his *other* girlfriend, and that's when he said he wouldn't have cheated on me if I was around more. That *I* had backed him into a corner where he had no other choice but to get his needs filled outside our relationship.'

Carlos's hand stopped halfway up her back before he slipped it around her waist and tightening as he pulled her closer to him, until her back was flush against his front. He nestled his face into her hair. Small fires exploded beneath her skin as he took a deep breath and hummed low.

'Did you believe him?' It was a question Sofia had heard before, though never in that tone. There wasn't any pity or bewilderment in his voice. Just an invitation to talk if she wanted it. And for the first time, she found that she *did* want to.

'For a while. It's much easier to find the fault in myself rather than admit that my partner could say such hurtful things just out of spite. We had promised to be truthful with each other, after all.' She shuddered when Carlos pressed a soft kiss to the back of her neck. 'Now I understand he acted out of pure selfishness, and that he did me a kindness with his behaviour. Now I know serious relationships can't survive the busy life of a trauma surgeon.'

A twitch went through the hand splayed over her stomach, but when Sofia looked down, it continued to draw circles on her skin as if there hadn't been an interruption. The question formed on her lips, wanting to know what he thought, but his lips against her skin turned the words in her throat into a quiet gasp.

'I'm glad you realised he's an idiot. And not just because your tattoo is gorgeous, but because of everything else on top of that grave insult,' Carlos said with his face still buried in her hair and trailing his lips over her neck.

Sofia didn't have anything to add to that and let herself be engulfed by the sensation his touches raked through her body. Lightness washed over her, one she hadn't sensed in a long time. She had thought herself pathetic for trusting Daniel. Had avoided talking about him because of the fear of being judged.

Sharing that side of her with Carlos was easy. Simple. Like she was *meant* to share herself like that. And it was the yearning bubbling up inside her that urged her to ask the next question— despite them having agreed not to get personal.

'Was it different for you and your wife? She knew what she had signed up for?'

'Mmm...' His hum was low and vibrated through

her skin into her body, where it settled in her core. 'My work could be a contentious topic from time to time—like any surgeon married to a non-physician.'

Sofia hadn't expected an answer—or the fireworks going off in the pit of her stomach at his words. Carlos was such a closed-off person, she'd begun combing through his sentences and anecdotes to trace them for any personal information. But he never slipped up, never said anything to hint at the life he'd lived before he left Brazil.

'But you must have found a solution to it?' she asked, though she wasn't sure why. A part of her wanted to know more about his marriage that had ended in his spouse's death.

'Sometimes,' he said, pressing a kiss behind her ear. His breath grazing over her cheek sent a shudder through her.

With each circle his fingers drew on her stomach, they wandered further down, and the closer they got to the apex of her thighs, the tighter the tension wound inside her. The curious part of her wanted him to stop and to talk more. But the part that hungered for him kept her tongue at bay, swallowing whatever questions she had as his hand reached between her thighs.

He had shared *something* with her, and even though Sofia knew she should be cautious, her heart beat faster at the tiny opening she'd spotted in his defences. Maybe with time they could figure something out. Because even though they had both agreed they would never have more than a casual encounter, Sofia didn't know how she could walk away from Carlos at the end of all this.

CHAPTER TEN

WAS IT POSSIBLE for life to feel the exact same way while being completely different? That thought followed Carlos around as he went about his days in the hospital. Because whether he wanted to admit it or not, Sofia had changed things inside of him—and the impact was far greater than he had anticipated.

Their desire for each other hadn't waned after their first night together, to the point where she had now spent most nights since then at his place, tangled up in his sheets. With that prospect to look forward to, it was easier to keep his hands to himself whenever he saw her at work. Easier, but not always possible. The explosiveness of their connection was unexpected and had made the time fly by. Now there were only a few days left on his contract before he would move on to his next assignment.

The affair wasn't supposed to change anything in his life, yet it had. With her gentle touch, her coaxing yet comforting words, and lips he wanted to feel on his skin for the rest of time, Sofia had pried open a door that had remained shut ever since Rosa passed away. But it wasn't the darkness of guilt and failed responsibilities flooding into him from that space. No, what came at him was light and warmth, the touch calm and soothing.

What that was supposed to mean, Carlos didn't know. The desire inside his chest was only growing with each passing day, with each stolen kiss they exchanged hidden away somewhere in the hospital—knowing that their final kiss was just around the corner.

Carlos would have served the length of his contract by the end of this week and was already busy writing up all of his documentation on the protocols he had implemented, as well as finishing some patient notes for a smooth handover. After that, the only other plan he had was a demonstration with the capoeira group during the Carnival days the following weekend.

'Cabrera.' He looked up from the computer screen when he heard his name and watched as Dr Sebastián Lopez approached him with a swift step. Though his gait was unhurried, something about him brought forth the feeling of unending tiredness. The bags underneath his eyes were more pronounced than when he'd last seen him some time ago.

'Chief Lopez,' he said with a nod, and got off his chair. 'Is everything okay?'

'Huh?' Sebastián came to a halt in front of his desk, his brows bunched as if he didn't understand his question.

'You look...tired.' Carlos surprised himself when he realised the concern in his voice was genuine. Had he ever cared about the staff in a hospital outside of what was professional courtesy? Because whatever was causing Sebastián sleepless nights most likely had nothing to do with work, or Carlos would have already heard about it.

'Oh... Yes. Since we're expecting triplets, Bella's pregnancy has been high-risk from the very start,' Sebastián said, glancing at his phone somewhat distractedly when it made a noise.

'It's been quite a while since my ob-gyn rotation during med school, but I remember triplets having a much higher chance of preterm birth,' Carlos said in an effort to sympathise with the man.

He let out another sigh, then put his phone away and straightened back up. 'I'm trying to reduce her hours even further, which she's not happy about. I'm not, either, because we're already short-staffed, and Bella is a menace when she has too much time on her hands and nothing to do with it.'

There was no harshness in his voice as he spoke of his wife. Only a quiet joy that shone through his words, and that sent a stab of guilt right into Carlos's chest. He remembered when he'd been the husband talking about his wife in the same tone. The accident had taken away his desire to talk about her. But as Sebastián kept speaking, a different need bubbled up in his chest now—prompting him to share something about himself, to keep building the connection between him and the other man.

Only problem was that what he wanted to share was about Sofia. About the time they had spent together. How her rich hair glistened in the moonlight as they had walked down the beach. That her smile lit the darker corners of his existence.

He shouldn't want any of this. It wasn't right, and he hadn't changed, either. He couldn't be the person someone like Sofia needed by her side—even though he knew the previous men in her life hadn't been deserving of her, either. Carlos wouldn't become one more on that list. He refused to drag her down.

'Anyway, that's not what I came here to discuss.' Sebastián paused, a thoughtful expression crossing his face. 'But thank you for asking. I appreciate that. You've integrated well with the staff, and the whole trauma department really came to like you.'

Carlos blinked at that sudden admission, not expecting it in the least. Sure, he had been friendly enough with the staff, but not overly close. His aim was always to instil the knowledge he needed to pass on without trying or wanting to be liked by the staff. Normally, half of them wouldn't be keen on him because he was the harbinger of change, forcing things onto them they weren't ready for. And he didn't get to bond with the other half who did like him because he usually left before he could form any meaningful connections.

Somehow, Sofia had managed to move from one group to the other, but also find a way into his heart to form the connection he usually fought off so vehemently.

'I'm glad to hear that. They have been a pleasure to teach,' he said, and the warmth trickling through his veins signalled to him that he actually meant those words. It was rare that he came to like a place he worked at as much as this— there just wasn't usually enough time to form an opinion. But even if he stepped back from his infatuation with Sofia, he had met people in and around the OR he genuinely enjoyed working with. The junior doctors were eager to learn, the nurses kind and attentive, and the more senior surgeons had all put in the effort to get on board with his plan.

'So…' Sebastián paused, his phone beeping again. He took it out of his pocket, staring at whatever news he had received. 'Shoot, I have to go. With Bella working even less, I'm now doing three people's jobs. What I actually came here for was to make you an offer.'

Carlos raised his eyebrows at his words. Something unspooled in the pit of his stomach, a ribbon of cold that drew itself through the warmth radiating across his body. There was only one offer Sebastián could make him.

'You probably get asked this at every place you go, but I would be mad not to ask you to stay. You've done great things with the team. The average surgery time is measurably down, and morale didn't take a hit with the implemented changes. I've spoken to the chief of surgery, and we have a position open for a senior surgeon. It's yours if you want it.'

'Thank you. I…' He stopped himself before he could go on, sensing that habit was driving him rather than his own intentions. He had received similar offers before at quite a few hospitals over the years, and he had always turned them down. Staying bound to one place wasn't something he had envisioned for his life ever since Rosa passed away. What good was settling down somewhere when all he had to look back on were broken promises?

But he would not automatically refuse this position as well. 'I appreciate the offer. When do you need to know my answer?'

Sebastián was already turning away as he spoke. 'Your contract is up in a few days, so let me know by then if you want to continue. Call my office for the detailed package for this role. You won't regret hearing it,' he said over his shoulder before disappearing into the bustle of the ER and leaving him to his own thoughts.

A role here at Hospital General? His heart had lurched at those words, and within one blink, a world of possibilities had unfolded in front of him. One where he could have the quiet warmth blooming inside of him for good—because Sofia was right there next to him. Meeting her had reintroduced something to his life he hadn't had in so long, and a part of him urged him to grab it with both hands and never let go. Never let *her* go.

But it wasn't that simple—even if Sofia made him want to believe it was. She was the reason his rejection to the job offer hadn't crossed his lips, why he was taking his time to consider it, even though he knew the answer needed to be no at the end. Sofia *couldn't* be the reason why he stayed, because how could he put such a monumental decision on her alone? How could he tell her that she was the reason he was even having to think about the offer? They had agreed whatever happened between them wasn't going to be anything serious.

When they began their affair, she had said she wasn't looking for anything long-term. Sofia had even been the one to make it clear from the very start that she couldn't be more to him than that. He had agreed with her, and wasn't even sure if what was happening deep inside of him was because he was changing. Or if he simply yearned to use her light to cast away the shadows. His mind was clouded, and separating his feelings from the reality of their situation became more of a struggle. Maybe it was for the best that he was leaving soon. That way he would escape even if he had already sunk way too deep into his messy feelings for Sofia.

She didn't want to be with him. That was what he clung to. And she wouldn't in future either, especially not if she knew about his involvement in his wife's death. No one in their right mind would stay with someone like him, so why risk the rejection?

Carlos was a man of principle. He wouldn't go back on his word to her and let her know how he felt—even if the thought of ending it and leaving her shredded his heart into even tinier pieces. It would be for the best. She was looking for far more than his broken self could ever give her.

* * *

'All right, thank you for presenting the case, Yasmine. Since we are on day two post-splenectomy, we should start him on prophylactic antibiotics and monitor him for any signs of postoperative complications,' Sofia said as she and the junior doctors in her care finished their rounds on the patients that had been through surgery in the last three days.

'What specific complications do we need to be vigilant about?' Yasmine asked, her pen hovering over the tiny notebook she carried around with her.

'After this surgery and the kind of accident he's been in, watch for anything out of the ordinary, but particularly respiratory distress or any signs of infection,' she replied.

Motion in her peripheral view drew her attention, and a smile spread over her lips when Carlos stepped out of an exam room with his own junior doctors. Snippets of their conversation drifted towards her, too quiet for her to understand any of the words. But the low rumble of his voice was enough to fill her head with memories of last night. And the night before. And all the nights before that.

'Good. Please update the patient charts before going down to the ER. Get your work assignments from the charge nurse there.' The gaggle of junior doctors around her dissolved, and Sofia walked back to the empty nurses' station, her eyes on Carlos, who looked down at the pager clipped to his waistband before moving towards the ORs at a hurried pace. An emergency? Sofia looked down at her own pager, but it remained silent. Probably another surgeon requesting his help.

Their whole entanglement had evolved beyond her expectations in every way. What had been intended as a quick release, a no-strings-attached affair, had become a form of companionship that had sneaked up on Sofia over the last week. Because they hadn't just gone to his place to sleep with each other. No, she had taken him around Buenos Aires, showing him her favourite corners. At times, they would just be quiet together, their fingers intertwined as they enjoyed the moment for what it was.

Was this really how these affairs evolved? Or had they slipped into something else, something more? That thought had bubbled up in her mind whenever they went out, when they held hands or lay in comfortable silence. But she had shut it down each time, not daring to even think about changing the terms of what they had already agreed on.

Still, Sofia had to recognise what had happened during their time together. In the hurt place in her heart that her past relationships had left behind now grew the seed of a new flower, tiny and fragile, hardly daring to poke its head out. But it was there, making her feelings for Carlos as real as their connection was.

How could she have fallen for someone she didn't even know? He'd talked to her about his wife, shared a sliver of the pain he must have felt, but outside of that one glimmer, Carlos had remained closed off to her. Sure, he had shared more of his past, talking about the hospitals he'd been in and what countries he had visited. But did she *really* know anything about him outside of that?

Despite not being able to list lots of things she knew about him, the feeling of deep connection remained. Could knowing a person really be boiled down to how many facts you knew about them? Or was it enough that Sofia knew he preferred orthopaedic work over cardiothoracic during surgery, and that he took a smaller scalpel size even for bigger incisions?

Was that enough to fall in love with someone?

She shook her head to disperse the thoughts, then checked the time before going to the cafeteria. Lulls in her schedule were few and far between, and she took the opportunity of some downtime to feed herself.

When she spotted Isabella sitting by herself,

she waved at her and smiled. Then she grabbed some food and sat down next to her friend. 'I haven't seen you around here in some time. Are you getting too big?' Sofia asked, her voice filled with affection for this woman.

Bella looked down at her, her hand patting her round belly. 'Sebastián won't let me do much while I carry these three around with me, and now he's teamed up with my ob-gyn to get me to do even more admin and less of the heavy work.'

Sofia laughed at the genuine indignation in the other woman's voice. 'How mean of them to give you sound medical advice and push you to take it.'

'I know they're right, but that doesn't change that I don't know what to do with myself outside of work.' Bella sighed, looking down at where her hand rested again. 'To be honest, I've not been feeling my best, either. But I would never admit that to Sebastián or he'll lock me up in the house. I'm still scheduled to help run the medical tent at Carnival, but I think I need to let Gabriel handle it. He says one of his childhood friends is a GP who's opening a clinic in the area, and she'll be there as well. But I hate to miss the action.'

'Don't remind me of the Carnival weekend. I already feel run down. The festivities always bring way too much traffic into the ER,' Sofia said, groaning at the thought. Though that wasn't the only thing filling her with unwanted dread. The beginning of Carnival also meant the end of her time with Carlos.

As if Bella read her mind, she narrowed her eyes. 'Are you looking forward to Dr Cabrera's final day?'

'What? No, why would you say that?'

'Sebastián said you didn't like him and that you two were constantly at each other's throats.' Bella shrugged when Sofia let out an indignant scoff.

'"At each other's throats" is overly dramatic, even for your husband. Since Carlos was so involved with teaching the junior doctors, I thought it only appropriate to give some feedback about his behaviour with them. I've known the juniors a lot longer than he has, after all,' she replied, and narrowed her eyes when a grin spread over her friend's lips. 'What?'

'You called him "Carlos",' she said, her eyes twinkling with delight.

Sofia willed her face to remain neutral as she replied, 'So? I call you and Sebastián by your first names.'

'Yeah, after we'd worked together for *two* years. And even then, we had to remind you regularly to be less formal with us. Cabrera has been here for how long? A month?' Isabella shook her head before levelling a more serious stare at her. 'Do you two intend to disclose your relationship to HR?'

This time Sofia couldn't keep her composure. Her eyes rounded at the casual tone Bella had employed. Not that she was wrong to ask the question. Technically they should have filled out a declaration, so the hospital was aware of any liabilities. Expect those rules were for *romantic* relationships, so she hadn't actually broken any rules. At least, that was the shred of truth she clung to.

'I'm not in a—'

'Stop right there, because there is no way you would lie to me like that,' Isabella interrupted her, holding up a hand in front of her.

Sofia bit down on her lower lip, glancing around her to make sure no one was paying too close attention to them, then leaned in to drop her voice to a quiet whisper. 'How could you possibly know that?'

'You two are way less subtle than you think you are. *Dios mío*, I saw him with his hand down your shirt, Fia.'

Flashbacks from that moment in the doctor's lounge came to her. 'I thought he had heard you in time to step away,' she said, then slapped her hand over her mouth when she realised she had just admitted Bella was right.

The satisfied flash in her friend's eyes told her she had noticed, too. 'No, I backed away and made sure to approach the lounge with more... audible steps,' she said. 'Sebastián thought something might be going on between you two as well. And I wouldn't be surprised if other people have noticed the steamy looks you've been giving each other across the ER.'

Steamy looks? Had they really let themselves get wrapped up in their affair so much that it had become obvious to everyone? Sofia hid her face behind her hands, releasing a quiet groan. But despite the embarrassment burning in her cheeks, her breaths came easier than they had in the last few weeks as a weight lifted off her. If Bella knew, then she finally had someone to talk to.

'It's not a relationship. It's a…situationship. He's leaving next week to who knows where, and I'll probably never see him again. Carlos has already been icing me out,' she said as she peeled her hands from her face.

Isabella tilted her head to the side. 'He's withdrawn from you?' she asked, and Sofia nodded.

Though each night still ended with them together, she sensed that his mind sometimes drifted away from the moments they shared, their conversations no longer flowing as freely as they used to. But whenever she asked him if something was the matter, he wouldn't respond—pulling her into a kiss or an embrace instead. Sofia had noticed this pattern in him before, whenever she'd asked him personal questions, and she understood that sometimes it was easier to express one's thoughts with touch and actions—but it was just as easy to avoid them in the same manner.

Was he trying to tell her something or avoiding having to open up to her?

The answer wasn't clear.

'I think it's because he's leaving soon and doesn't want to drag things out. We said this would only be about sex.'

'And is it?'

Sofia paused, the word 'yes' getting stuck in her throat. Bella had caught her earlier lie with such ease, she didn't believe she could get away with another one. One that was far closer to her heart. So she shook her head, her gaze dropping down to where her hands began fiddling with the plastic cup of water to release some of the nervous tension.

'Nope… I've caught feelings for him, and now I'm an emotional mess because I wasn't supposed to fall in love with him.' She resisted the urge to hide behind her hands again as the tension flowed out of her. There they were. The words she'd been dreading saying finally spilled out into the open.

Isabella's expression softened at her words, at the quiet agony she was sure the other woman could hear. Sofia had fallen in love with the one man she'd promised not to, and there was no way out of the web he'd spun around her.

'Obviously, I have no hope of ever being with him, so I just have to…wait for it to pass.' Waiting for that tiny spot of light in her chest to sputter out.

'Why do you have no hope of ever being with him?'

Sofia paused, her brow furrowing. Was that some kind of trick question? 'Because…he's leaving the hospital.'

'Ah yes…' Isabella breathed out, and Sofia almost missed the hint of an expression on her face. But she'd worked with her long enough to understand all her friend's non-verbal cues that were essential for a good working relationship in high-pressure environments like an ER.

Sofia leaned further in. 'Bella… What aren't you telling me?'

The other woman shook her head. 'Nothing that should concern you,' she replied, her mouth thin as she pressed her lips together.

'Spit it out. I told you my secret. You owe me one.' Her heart beat against her chest in an uneven stutter as her mind came up with all the worst-case scenarios. Was Carlos already gone? Had he told the hospital leadership about their 'situationship'?

Isabella glanced around. 'After talking to the chief of surgery about the results we're seeing in the OR, Sebastián offered Carlos a permanent position here.'

Sofia's eyes rounded. The chief wanted Carlos to stay? Did Carlos want that, too? The lack of knowledge she possessed about this man came rushing back at her when she found herself unable to predict how he would react. She was almost certain that his late wife was the reason he didn't stay in Brazil, but did it mean he had to keep moving?

'What did he say?' Sofia almost didn't dare to ask that question. Because if she learned that he'd declined the offer straight away, that small ray of hope would fade into nonexistence when she had only just now admitted to it. Would he really not talk to her about this before making a decision? Okay, she wasn't his girlfriend, but did she really mean that little to him?

'Apparently he said—'

A shrill beep interrupted Isabella, and Sofia looked down as she unclipped the pager from her waistband. Her blood chilled when she read the message on the small screen.

911-OR 2-Dr CC-pressure.

Pressure? Carlos was under pressure in OR Two? What kind of emergency was he dealing with that he had to…

Sofia jumped from her chair when the meaning of the message clicked into place. Pressure. Carlos was having a panic attack during surgery.

'I have to go,' she said, hurrying to pick up the chair where it had clattered to the floor from her sudden jolt upright.

'Wait, do you not want to know—'

'No time. Carlos needs me in the OR.' The content and direction of their conversation were wiped from Sofia's mind, along with any of her inner turmoil as she sprinted towards the surgical floor—towards Carlos.

CHAPTER ELEVEN

CHAOS ERUPTED AROUND her when Sofia entered the OR, and her eyes widened as she assessed the scene. Carlos had his hand in the chest of the patient, counting evenly under his breath as his arm moved. Was he performing a cardiac massage?

Her silent question was answered when he took his arm out, and the surgeon assisting him inserted the paddles of an internal defibrillator into the chest cavity. Everyone stood back from the patient, who only slightly bowed off the table when the electricity jolted through her.

The monitor continued to emit a flat tone. Sofia stepped closer to the patient as Carlos's hand went back to do the cardiac massage. She could see his chest rising and falling in a faster than normal rhythm. His skin looked pale and sweaty, his eyes focused on whatever his hands were doing. Something during the surgery had triggered him, and this was the result.

'How long has the patient been in asystole?' Sofia asked the anaesthetist sitting at the head of the patient, who wore a look of concern on her face.

'Eleven minutes.'

'What about a pupil response?' She watched as the anaesthetist got up from her chair, slipping a small penlight out of her pocket and lifting the closed lids of the patient. She checked the patient's eyes, then shook her head.

'Palpable pulse anywhere?' Sofia looked at the junior doctor this time, who set the paddles down to check for a pulse at various locations on the body before stepping away with another headshake.

Glancing at the tray to the side of the anaesthetist, she could see they had administered several rounds of epinephrine without getting any results, either. Her heart clenched when she looked towards Carlos, who was still performing a cardiac massage and not willing to give up—even though the patient had.

'Dr Cabrera,' she called out, putting as much steel in her voice as she dared without plunging him deeper into whatever cycle he was descending into. She needed to get him out of this situation. 'We've lost the patient. She's gone. Please call the time of death so we can inform her next of kin.'

Carlos slowed the squeezing of his hand, looking up at Sofia through eyes that were struggling to stay in the moment. But he heard her, which was a good sign. She could get through to him and ground him. 'I will call it,' she said softly, intending the words only for his ears.

When he nodded, she swallowed the sigh of relief and looked at the clock hanging on the wall. 'Time of death is 17:21,' she announced, then looked at the junior doctor. 'Go update the chart and then find out if her next of kin is already here. If so, just tell them that the surgeon will be out to update them shortly. We'll take care to close her up.' She looked at the anaesthetist with her last sentence, who nodded and flipped the switches on the monitor before gathering her things and leaving.

When the doors to the OR swung shut and they were alone, Sofia circled around to Carlos's side. 'You paged me with the word "pressure" because you sensed the panic attack incoming, didn't you?'

Carlos's breath came fast, his hands finally ceasing their attempt at resuscitation, and they fell to his sides. 'She's... I couldn't help her, and she—' His words faded into a mumble she couldn't understand, and Sofia swallowed her mounting concern to focus on calming him. Embracing him was out of the question in their situation or they might risk contaminating each other.

'Okay, let's try to ground you. I have brushed

up on PTSD-induced panic attacks since the last time. I know you must be familiar with the five-four-three-two-one technique.' She paused, wrapping her hands around his wrists and pulling him towards her and away from the patient until he could only see Sofia.

'Tell me about five things you can see,' she prompted him.

His eyes darted around, and Sofia strengthened her grip around his wrists to keep him from turning. Whatever had triggered him had to do with the patient. She didn't want him looking anywhere else until she had pulled him out of this panic attack.

'The heart rate monitor, the yellow biohazard waste bin, the OR lights, my hands…your hands.' He said each word slowly and with deliberation, moving from left to right as he named the objects he could see. The rate of his breathing decreased, and Sofia squeezed his wrists again with as much pressure as she could.

'Now look for four things you can touch,' she said to continue the exercise.

His hands curled into fists as his gaze dropped down. 'With your hands around my wrists, I can only touch me and you,' he said, though his voice came through steadier than before.

'I know you're supposed to touch, but there is only so much you can do with gloves. Just observe what you *could* touch if you needed to,' she replied, loosening her grip slightly.

'The heart rate monitor, the instrument tray, myself and you.' Then his hands slackened again, his palms turning upwards. 'Is the family here? I need to…speak to them.'

Her heart squeezed tight at his question. Even through his panic attack, he still tried to think of his patient first.

'You're not in any shape to talk to the family, Carlos. They just lost someone dear to them. Their grief won't help with your panic.' Though she understood his desire to speak to the family, the part inside her that cared way too deeply for his well-being and happiness wanted to shield him from the experience—even if she knew that as a doctor, he had to tell the family what had happened in his OR. 'Now tell me three things you can hear.'

'The ticking of the clock, the rustling of our gowns, your voice.' Sofia paused, her eyes still on his, not sure if she should continue. She worried about the next step—naming two things he could smell. Because as with any long surgery, the sterile scent of the OR had been replaced with the coppery tang of blood. If his senses grabbed onto that, his panic might rise all over again.

'Are you able to move?' She breathed out a sigh of relief when Carlos nodded, and she led him to the biohazard bin he had named a few moments ago to discard their gloves and gowns before pushing him out the door into the scrub room.

'I'll page one of the trainees to come and close her up,' Sofia said, and not even a second later, the door swung open as the doctor who'd been assisting Carlos came back in.

'The family is here, Dr Martinez. They're waiting in the meeting room,' he said, and Sofia gave him a grateful nod.

'Please close the patient up and get her transported to a room so they can see her when they're ready. I'll go inform the family.'

Carlos stretched his hand out when she moved to walk past him, grabbing her by the arm. 'She's my patient. I should be the one to tell them,' he said, and even though she knew he was trying hard to calm himself, she could still hear the slight wobble in his voice. Whatever he wanted anyone to think, she *knew* he was not fine.

But she couldn't disagree with him in front of the staff, or she might accidentally reveal his diagnosis. So she nodded, but followed him out the door.

There was only one meeting room on their floor, and it was reserved for the times they needed to talk to families of patients who hadn't made it through surgery. Carlos had never dreaded going into that room to have the tough conversation—until this moment.

He'd received the page to go to OR Two for an emergency surgery. Since all the other surgeons were occupied, he'd had to cut his rounds short to rush to the operating room. A pang of nerves had fluttered in the pit of his stomach as he pushed the doors open, and when he saw the unconscious woman lying on the operating table, the all-too-familiar sound of his blood rushed through his ears.

Unlike many other times when he'd had to work through rising panic while treating a patient who reminded him of Rosa, this time the grounding techniques had failed to keep him from slipping into the blackness of his panic attack. He'd kept it at bay for the majority of the surgery until it became clear that the damage to the patient was too great for them to fix it—and he was once again confronted with his powerlessness.

Another person he couldn't save. How many did that make?

As the blackness had crept in, he'd had the foresight to page Sofia with a code word he hoped she would understand. He'd retreated from her in the last few days as his last shift at Hospital General de Buenos Aires approached, but though he'd kept her at arm's length during the day, his resolve had crumbled whenever he spotted her on the way out—and they'd ended up at his place over and over again.

Twice now had he relied on Sofia to pull him out of a sticky situation, and he wondered why he had such a poor grip on his symptoms when they hadn't been that hard to manage in the past. He took his medication religiously, needing it to function in the high-stress environment of a hospital.

Was it because of his closeness to Sofia? Though it had ebbed and flowed in the years since Rosa's death, the guilt over what had happened remained his steady companion, reminding him to never be that careless again—to keep people out because *he* couldn't be trusted to have them. The pain he had grown so used to had dulled, sometimes even fading away altogether when he was with Sofia— and a small part of him had begun to wonder what would happen if he let her in.

That he would want her as much as he did had not been part of the plan. And that inner turmoil had his nerves stretched so thin, they were close to snapping—and had finally done so during surgery.

Yet Sofia had been the one to fix it…

Nausea roiled in his stomach as he stood in front of the closed door of the meeting room, running the script of what to say in his head. This was just like any other bad outcome, the words exactly the same ones he had said many times over. This was not Rosa, and he wouldn't stand face-to-face with her parents as he told them what happened.

No, behind those doors waited the parents of Valentina Alvarez.

'Are you okay?' Sofia stood behind him, close enough for him to sense the warmth from her body radiating into his back.

He shook his head, inhaling while he counted and then repeating the same on the exhale. He was not okay, and he never would be. These last few weeks had almost convinced him that he might have a normal life again, that he might find it within himself to love again—to let a woman like Sofia love him in return. But he couldn't do it. No matter how much he wished otherwise.

The blackness of his panic came rushing back in with a vengeance that stole all the breath from his lungs. The deep breaths became shallow, and his eyes darted around in search of something to anchor him, but the edges of his vision blurred with each passing second until the world became shapeless and vague around him.

'Carlos, honey...' Sofia must have sensed something, for she put her hand on his shoulder, giving it a reassuring squeeze. A spark travelled down that arm, but fizzled out before he could grasp it. It had been bound to happen. Nothing could take root when faced with the overwhelming guilt inside of him.

'Could...you please speak to the family? I can't do it.' Her grip on him tightened as he admitted to this failure. The words tasted bitter on his tongue, but his muscles were seizing up at the thought of going into that room, his throat almost too tight to speak the words he had just said.

'Of course.' There was nothing but understanding in her voice, and that just threw him further into the pit he found himself in. Would she be this sympathetic towards him if she knew what he had done? That it was his fault his wife had died? He doubted she would find that much compassion in her heart for him if she knew. Maybe she would even regret having met him at all...

'Thanks.' He mumbled the word before shaking her hand off his shoulder to find a place in the hospital where the air wasn't so thick he could choke—like he was choking right now.

Despite only coming in at the end of the surgery, Sofia felt confident in giving the parents of Valentina Alvarez all the information about what had happened to their daughter—and providing as much compassion as she could. It wasn't easy to be the bearer of bad news, and she had never let herself get complacent enough to become used to being the messenger. But emergency medicine produced more bad outcomes than any other discipline, so talking to a distraught family was a regular part of her job.

She'd put the moment with Carlos to the back of her mind, pushing it down into a little compartment where it would sit untouched until she had the time to deal with it. It was a skill she'd learned early in her training as a trauma surgeon. Even in the OR, she needed to compartmentalise different concurrent emergencies to focus on the place that needed most of her attention.

Now that she had left the family to grieve, she could get back to Carlos—and what had happened to him. Something inside her had told her he still wasn't well when they stepped out of the OR, despite his assurances that he was fit to speak to the family. That instinct had her sticking close to him, and the nearer they got to the room where the family waited for them, the more signs of another panic attack looming appeared on his body.

Without thinking, Sofia let her feet carry her to the ER, where she now stood in front of the supply closet in which they had shared several moments. She wasn't sure if he'd ever disclosed his condition to the hospital administration, and she'd figured it was none of her business. Up to this day, it hadn't interfered with patient care. But now that it had, something inside of her cracked.

She had to tell Sebastián, didn't she? Sure, Carlos was leaving in a few days, but a lot could happen in that time span. What if he had another panic attack, and she wasn't here to help him?

But before she spoke to the chief, she'd talk to Carlos first. Give him the chance to do it himself.

Taking a deep breath to steel her resolve, Sofia pushed the door handle down, slipped through the open crack of the door, and then locked it behind her. What she found inside wrenched at her heart.

Carlos sat on a box stacked on the floor, his hand bracing his forehead as he stared down at the floor. His breath was steadier than she had expected, showing some signs of calm, but sweat still gleamed on his skin, which lacked its usual vibrancy. The exact hue of his skin had become so ingrained in her memory that any small deviation appeared huge in her mind.

'Carlos…' She sank to the floor in front of him, sitting down cross-legged so her knees were touching his shins. 'Are you doing okay?'

She asked the question, knowing full well he wasn't anywhere near okay, and was wrestling with a lot of different emotions. Asking if he was okay felt wholly inadequate for the situation they were in, but she lacked any other words to express herself…except maybe the truth? 'I'm worried about you.'

Carlos let out a sharp exhale, his eyes squeezing shut for several breaths before he raised his head to look at her. 'It seems to be worse here than in other hospitals I've worked in, and I have asked myself why. Female car crash victims in their twenties are a trigger for me because of Rosa, but I've *always* kept my composure in past situations. Not once did anyone have to rescue me in my own surgery.'

Rosa? Was that his wife? Had they been in a car accident that resulted in her death? A shudder ran through Sofia at the thought, and how often he had to expose himself to the same traumatic event as a surgeon working in emergency medicine.

'Are you in treatment for your panic disorder?' Even though she wanted to know more about Rosa, she swallowed any questions bubbling up. She craved that information, but she wouldn't want to get it when he wasn't at his best.

He gave a terse nod, his gaze dropping back to the floor. 'My psychiatrist is in Brazil. I haven't seen him in a while, but my medication works just fine, so there was no reason to keep seeing him.'

Sofia stretched out a hand, gently wrapping it around his calf. 'Maybe it's not working any more if your panic attacks are increasing. If the severi—'

'My panic attacks are increasing because I *killed* my wife, and now I'm trying to move on with my life like it had never happened. I have let myself think that I can be happy again—that I could be deserving of someone's affection after so long.' The words poured forth with an intensity that rippled through her.

Sofia's blood ran cold as she processed what he had said. The hurt etched into his voice tore at her skin, leaving her breathless for a few moments as the meaning of what he'd just said settled between them. He had done what…?

The rational side of her brain kicked in, and she forced her own anxiety into a box so she could focus on one thing at a time. There was no way he had done anything to his late wife or he wouldn't be sitting across from her right now. Sofia might not know a lot about Carlos or his past, but she knew the person he was deep down inside.

'Your panic attacks are triggered by the victims of motor vehicle accidents. Were you the driver?' she asked as she put her thoughts in order.

Carlos took a deep breath and nodded. 'We were on our way home from…somewhere. I can't remember the details any more, only that it was later than usual. We were having an argument, and then everything just went…dark.'

The brittleness in his voice was a sound Sofia had never heard from him, and it tore at her along with the pain contorting his face. She didn't know what to say, didn't have enough details to comfort him or give him a new perspective—though she still doubted he was truly responsible for what he was describing.

'I woke up at the hospital to the news that a drunk driver had hit the passenger side of the car as we crossed an intersection and that Rosa was killed instantly,' he continued, a deep exhale leaving his body as he said those words.

Her hand remained wrapped around his calf, squeezing it now and then to signal to him that she was still here—still listening. The extent of his trauma hit her, and all the disjointed things she knew about Carlos fused together to reveal the larger picture of who he was. There was no family waiting for him in Brazil because Rosa had been that family, and he spent his time travelling from place to place because he was untethered. Sofia had believed him to be a charming playboy, having a different woman in each city he visited, but she couldn't have been more wrong.

Was she the first person to grab his attention since his wife passed away? The thought sent conflicting waves of heat and cold through her. Sofia didn't want to believe the feeling rising within her, the desperate hope that maybe he felt the same way about her as she did about him.

'A drunk driver hit you from the side and you blame yourself?' The words sounded harsher than she intended, more like a criticism than a genuine question. Carlos's head snapped back up to level a stare at her, and her breath hitched at the steel in his eyes.

'I was distracted, arguing about something I can't even remember. What if there had been any warning signs? Maybe I could have heard the car coming if only...' His voice trailed off as he shook his head.

'If you were treating such a patient in the ER, would you agree with that? Because I think you would point out how powerful survivor's guilt can be in distorting what really happened.' She didn't back down from his gaze.

'So you're just another person telling me what I have seen and felt and experienced isn't true—isn't *valid*.' Sofia took a breath, steadying herself as the words found their mark. She knew what he was doing, knew he was seeking validation for the narrative that kept him from letting people get too close to him.

'What I'm saying is that I understand you have a long way to go until you can forgive yourself. I'm telling you that I see you for who you are—a brilliant and compassionate man, who struggles with his demons like many of us.' Sofia unfolded her legs, twisting them behind her until she was on her knees and close to eye level with him. Her breath shook, but her hands remained steady as she reached out, framing his face with her hands.

Carlos took a sharp breath, but he didn't pull away. Her thumbs stroked over his cheekbones, each sweep sending a tingle down her arms. 'I'm saying that I see both the light and dark in you. I see it all, and I still want you.'

A stuttering sigh left her as the words she'd been longing to say flowed out of her. The truth hung between them, but Sofia wasn't scared of it. She thought she would have been, had believed Daniel had caused so much damage to her heart and soul that she would never recover. But staying away from the man she loved, from a future with him just because she'd been burned before, was exactly the thing she *shouldn't* do. The best revenge would be to lead her best life. And she would always question if that life could have included Carlos if she didn't have enough courage to ask.

She leaned in so that their noses touched, leaving some distance between them to give him a choice. She didn't have to wait long until he closed the gap between them, sliding his mouth over hers. Tranquillity washed over her as his lips moved against hers, as his familiar taste and scent thundered through her. Everything inside of her relaxed as the positive answer sunk into her mind. He was choosing her, too.

Elation carried her away into the clouds—and then her stomach swooped as she fell out of them when Carlos wrenched his mouth away and stood up, putting distance between them. Her heart cracked under the regretful expression on his face as he shook his head. 'I can't be… I'm not free to give myself to you, Sofia.' His throat worked as he looked at her, and each breath he took looked to be as much of a struggle as hers felt.

'There's a reason I don't stay anywhere longer than a few months, including here. It's because…' His voice trailed off, his hand balling into a fist. Sofia could see the mental battle going on, of whether he should trust her with whatever was going on. Was that why they were doomed to fail? Because even now, when she'd seen him broken down, he still hesitated?

'Because you need to keep running away from your problems. I get it.' She couldn't keep the bitterness out of her words—didn't even try. Agreement or not, she had put herself out there for him to hold on to if he wanted. Which, as it turned out, he didn't. She pushed past him and pulled the door open, but then paused to look at him. 'Ever wonder why your problems are already there waiting for you whenever you arrive at a new place?'

Then she turned around and walked away, her heart tearing in two with every step that took her away from the man she loved.

CHAPTER TWELVE

WHY WAS THE ER so quiet? Sofia would never dare to speak these words out loud lest she summoned some catastrophe to their doors. Though she wasn't superstitious, she knew there were important rules for keeping the harmony in the emergency room—and she didn't want to be the person to disrupt it.

The surgical board was empty, the ambulance bay quiet, and even the doctors in the ER didn't need her help. She found herself strolling down the corridor towards the trauma bays once more, poking her head into each one to ask if they needed any assistance. Two were empty, one was being cleaned, and in the last one she found Sebastián in exactly the same position as the previous time she came by twenty-odd minutes ago—hunched over his laptop and staring at the screen.

'Are you haunting my ER?' he asked without looking up, and Sofia chose to interpret his words as an invitation to join him.

She hopped onto the exam table, sitting next to

where the chief had his laptop. 'Don't you have an office to work from?'

'With Bella taking it easy, I have to pick up the slack on admin work and actual emergency medicine work, so it's easier to tuck myself away in a corner here and wait to be needed than run across the hospital several times a day,' he said. When Sofia lifted her hands to indicate the empty space around her, he shot her a warning look. 'Don't say it.'

'I wasn't going to! And here I thought I was in a bad mood, but you can have it all to yourself.' The moment she admitted to her bad mood, regret set in, and she prayed Sebastián wouldn't be nosy enough to ask her about it. She was almost certain he knew already. If Bella had noticed what went on between her and Carlos, then she would have told her husband.

'I think the same person put us in a bad mood,' Sebastián replied, and she raised her eyebrows at that.

'Huh? What did Carlos do to you?' Ever since their fight in the supply closet, Sofia hadn't seen much of him at the hospital. They were avoiding each other, which was working rather well. She'd asked the charge nurse to page her instead of him with any motor vehicle accidents coming in, and had left Carlos alone to do whatever he needed to before leaving Buenos Aires. Before forgetting about what had happened between them.

She couldn't forget though—not once she had peered into the Pandora's box that was her wealth of feelings for him. So instead, she had spent the last few days convincing herself that she wasn't capable of a casual *or* serious relationship at this point in her life. Because what was supposed to have been casual had developed into serious far quicker than she'd anticipated—and just like with Daniel, she was now alone again to pick up the pieces.

'He refused the hospital's offer of a permanent position. I'm not surprised he did, but that still leaves us with too few surgeons and ER doctors alike.' He shot her a glance. 'What happened between you two? Just last week, you were glued to each other.'

Sofia let out a groan as the memories of their confrontation came back—along with the feelings inside her chest. Had they really been that obvious with their affection for one another? Everyone had noticed and yet he'd still rejected her?

'It wasn't anything serious. We just got a bit carried away with all the…sex.' Because that was what it had been, right? Nothing more than the two of them enjoying each other's company without any strings attached. Though she didn't quite know how Sebastián had suddenly become her confidant, so she quickly added, 'Not that you want to hear about that.'

To her surprise, he closed the laptop and leaned back to look up at her, his hands folded in front of him. 'You know Bella and I struggled in our marriage. It took us quite a while to find our way back to each other. Why don't you humour me?'

'What's there to say? I'm sure your wife already gave you an update on what happened after I told her all about Carlos. You couldn't have told me that we were being so painfully obvious?' She replayed certain moments in time where she had believed them to be unobserved, but now she wondered how many people had actually seen them together. Not that it mattered. He was gone now.

'You two were *trying* to be discreet. Who am I to burst that bubble for you?' he asked with a shrug.

'The chief of emergency medicine? Shouldn't you be the first one to discourage a secret relationship between two staff members?' Sofia wasn't certain why she was arguing against her own case. Maybe the blatant disregard for the rules was finally catching up with her. Maybe that's why they hadn't worked out...

Sebastián called her out. '*Now* you care about the rules? But while you were having fun, you didn't care all that much? Sofia...' He shook his head. 'I'm not *your* chief, but I do see him every day, and I can assure you that he would have as little of a problem as I do if you two made things official.'

Did she want to be with Carlos? She had told him so, had offered up her heart, only for him to walk away from it—from her. Just like every other man in her life had. Not a single one had stuck through the trouble, stayed with her and figured out how to bridge the gaps. It broke her heart that she had to put Carlos on that list, too. He knew her life as a surgeon, knew her insecurities, and had always—*always*—ensured she was in a comfortable place. Whether that was dancing at the bar or making love back at his flat. He'd shown her how much he treasured her, only to walk away when she wanted to give it all back to him.

'He didn't want that. I...told him that I wanted him, but he said he wasn't interested,' she said after a stretch of quiet, reluctant to dip back into that particular memory.

'Did you tell him you loved him?' Sofia's head whipped around to look at Sebastián at the unexpected question.

'What? No, I didn't.'

Sofia buried her face in her hands, letting out a frustrated groan. 'I do love him, but I shouldn't. I've only known him for a month.'

'I've seen crazier things happen. You two went through several stressful surgeries together, and you've challenged him every time you thought he could do better. I can see why he fell in love with you,' Sebastián said with a casual shrug, but his words sent a trickle of hot and cold sensations racing down her spine.

'He's not in love with me, and he said as much when I poured my heart out to him,' she replied in an immediate defence. Sebastián raised his hands.

'I wasn't there, but Bella and I have both seen you struggle through some pretty bad relationships where you were trying to make yourself fit into a mould when you really should be with someone who appreciates you as you are. Cabrera was the first person to be your equal, where you didn't have to change anything about you to fit perfectly together—because from day one he saw you for who you are.' He paused, his fingers tapping on his closed laptop in a gesture she'd seen many times from him whenever he considered what to say next. 'Daniel really messed you up. We were all there for the fallout, and I think a part of you still believes that you have to choose between work and love. But you don't. The moment you're brave enough to let go of the hurt you're clinging to, you will see that—and then you'll tell him how you feel.'

Let go? Sofia leaned back until she was lying

down on the exam table, staring up at the fluorescent lights glaring above her. Had she been carrying the hurt around for so long, never finding a place where she could bury it for once and for all? She knew deep inside that Sebastián was right, or his words wouldn't have shaken her as much as they had. With Daniel, she had believed she'd found someone that could run parallel to her life, who understood enough of her passion as a surgeon to accept the long hours, the abandoned dates and everything else that came with it.

But instead of being honest with her and telling her things weren't working out, he had taken it upon himself to get his needs met elsewhere. Carlos wasn't a dishonest person. In the depths of her heart, she knew that. If she told him how she felt, would his answer remain the same? Or was this the crucial piece of information missing for him to be able to make a decision?

'Am I letting my past experiences interfere with my life this much?' she asked out loud, needing to get the swirling voices out of her head.

'Of course you are. Who doesn't? That's how we learn not to touch the stovetop while it's still hot. We learn from our mistakes. But there's learning how to stand up for yourself better and then there's not even trying because it *might* hurt,' Sebastián replied, and his words shifted something into place that Sofia had already known for a while—yet had not wanted to acknowledge.

Because she was as scared that her involvement with Carlos could end in something spectacular as she was of it going just like any other relationship. She didn't *want* it to be like her previous relationships because that was how much he already meant to her. If Sebastián was right about that, could he also be right about Carlos loving her too?

'Do you know if he already left Argentina?' she asked when a tentative plan formed in her head.

'Sorry, I don't know anything about his future plans. Don't you have his phone number?'

Sofia did, but ever since that final moment in the supply closet, their text chain had remained quiet. Her fingers hovered over the keyboard more often than she cared to admit, but each attempt at a message had resulted in not a single word sent. But even if he was still in Buenos Aires, it was the first day of Carnival, and—

'I know where he is…' she breathed out, bolting upright and jumping off the table with a sudden burst of energy. 'He'll be at Carnival, at least for today. But… I have to stay here.'

This time Sebastián raised his hands—and one eyebrow—to indicate the almost silent ER around them. 'And what exactly are you going to miss here?'

Sofia sucked in a breath. 'But I get into trouble for even suggesting that it might be too qu—'

'You can hint at it, but you can't say the word, Martinez.' He shook his head in mock disapproval. 'Go find him and bring him back. He has transformed our efficiency like nothing else. I *want* him back. If there's an emergency coming in that we aren't able to handle with the junior doctors, I'll page you.'

She stared at him, processing his words, not quite sure if he meant it. Could she really leave, or was that just asking for trouble? Not that there was anything for her to do in the ER. All the injuries coming in were minor scrapes, bruises and a lot of alcohol poisoning. Nothing that needed a surgeon to help.

'Okay,' she said with a nod, her resolve firming. 'I will bring him back.'

Carnival was an explosion of colour and sound that swept Sofia up the second she stepped into the fray. The main procession wound its way down the main street, following the predetermined course from one side of the city to the other. Dancers stood on their floats, their costumes bright and loud as they flowed through their dance steps to the music playing from the speakers. People with drums and maracas stood amidst the spectators, filling the air with a beat that blended seamlessly with the notes the many troupes were playing just a few steps down. Though they were all following their own beat, somehow it blended together into an upbeat sound that embodied the Carnival vibes of Buenos Aires.

How long had it been since Sofia had come here just to enjoy herself? She couldn't answer the question, only remembering how much time she had spent in the OR on these days.

Carlos wouldn't be on one of the floats. He'd told her the capoeira group he belonged to would be performing their usual exhibition *jogos* at the Carnival to drum up some interest in their gym. Apparently most of their new members joined them because of Carnival. But knowing enough about capoeira now, she understood that they wouldn't be able to do their *jogos* on something that moved as much as a motorised float. No, they had to be one of the many dance and entertainment groups spilling over to the side streets.

Would it be hard to spot them? Sofia looked around her as she combed through the streets lined with food stands and collections of furniture people had pulled out of their flats nearby so everyone could sit together.

They would be forming a large circle of white-clad people, so surely this would catch her attention immediately? At least she really hoped it would. Nervous fingers went back to the pager on her waistband, making sure she hadn't missed anything from the ER. Though there were enough junior surgeons still around to consult, she was the senior person they relied on.

Standing at small crossroads, Sofia cast her glance everywhere. Her step faltered when she saw someone in flowing white linen trousers sitting down on a chair underneath a tented area. A flag hung from the roof of the tent, a white background with a green cross on it. The medical tent.

A smile tugged at her lips when she recognised who was approaching the man sitting on the chair. So Gabriel was in charge of the medical tent? Bella must have asked him to step in for her, like she said she was going to. Then a woman in a wheelchair came into view, looking up at the paramedic before asking the man in the chair a question. Sofia furrowed her brow as she watched them. That must be the GP Bella had mentioned—Gabriel's childhood friend. Sofia wondered what her name was.

She squinted, trying to see the badge clipped to her scrub top, but then the man in the chair lifted his hand and pointed down one of the roads. Sofia perked up. The style of clothes he wore was unmistakable, and she was sure he was part of the capoeira troupe.

She glanced at her phone as she walked in

the direction indicated, looking at the hour and checking for any messages from Sebastián. There wasn't much time until she was needed back at the hospital. Determined to find Carlos, she increased her pace, gazing up and down the little alleyways where people were drinking, dancing and celebrating, until she finally spotted the circle of white shirts and trousers along with the now familiar sound of the berimbau and atabaque droning a low and rhythmic beat for the *capoeiristas*.

She stepped closer. Her breath hitched when she saw Carlos leave the *roda* to enter the *jogo*. Luckily for her, he had decided to keep his shirt on, and she smiled when she recognised the logo of the gym emblazoned in dark red on the otherwise white shirt. He moved like he wasn't made out of flesh and bone, but rather a liquid he could form at his will, bending to dodge his opponent and then snapping back.

The control he showed during capoeira extended to the rest of his life, Sofia realised as she watched him. They had been going back and forth in their own *jogo*, each one giving as much as they took, weaving in and out of each other's space without their lives ever truly touching. They had both done it to avoid letting the other one get too close. Her because of Daniel and how he had wrecked her confidence, and him because no one had ever shown him that he was still deserving of love and tenderness in the face of loss.

This would stop now. Sofia would either succeed in laying her heart out for real, making him see everything there was between them—or she would leave here at the very least knowing she had tried to touch his heart. Even if the whole point of their affair had been not to.

Sweat dripped down his brow as Carlos dropped low to avoid a kick, then used the momentum to surge back up and cartwheel to the side as the third *capoeirista* engaged the *jogo*. Then he caught a glimpse of a familiar pair of golden eyes watching him. But before he could process that, he was drawn back into the game, and the cheers around them grew louder.

Was she...? He spun around again, scanning the crowd, but none of them—

His eyes widened when he saw Sofia standing behind the first row of white-clad people, looking at him with an adoration so intense it hit him straight in the stomach—causing him to lose his footing on the next step. He still evaded his opponent's strike, but had to fall backwards and catch himself with his hands. Using the momentum, he pushed himself into a handstand and then flipped backwards to land near the edge of the *roda*, where he tagged someone else in to take his place.

Sofia was here, and the need to know why burned through him. Why would she seek him out again after their last encounter?

Ever since pushing her away, Carlos had tossed and turned in his bed each night, trying to deny to himself how much he missed her. How every day he woke up by himself had been worse for exactly that reason. But he couldn't admit—couldn't accept—how deeply Sofia had dug into his heart, finding the place he had guarded so closely for the last five years, and settling in there with grace and ease. As if she had been born with the key to that door in her hand.

But he couldn't let her wield that key. Not when his heart still bled from the last time, the guilt still gnawing at him whenever he sought it out. He couldn't…yet the last month had brought his soul back to life like nothing—*no one*—else had. Sofia was…everything. Everything he wanted from someone in his life. A person who challenged him, who held him to the same high standards as he had for other people. She was passionate about her work, quick on her feet in the OR, and when their bodies moved against each other—be it on the bed or on the dance floor—he could hear the song of the stars moving through the universe.

Carlos knew he had lost his heart to her the first time they'd danced together in that bar. With her body pressed against his, he could not only see the expression on her face change, but also feel how her muscles relaxed against him with each step. The spark in her eyes that had appeared when she had figured out the right steps had almost undone him there and then. In that moment, he had realised it was over for him—he was in love with this woman.

So pushing her away had been one of the hardest things he'd had to do to save her from himself. Since she had been avoiding him at the hospital, he had thought it had worked. Yet here she stood, gazing at him with unveiled longing that pressed so hard against his chest, he was sure his ribs were about to cave in.

Carlos pushed his way through the crowd, then followed the circle of people until he stood face-to-face with her. His muscles seized up, tension rippling through his body as his mind projected the million different conversations that could happen in this moment. There was only one conversation he *wanted* to have, even though he wasn't allowed to yearn for it. Between now and last week, nothing had changed. He still had too much to atone for to let her into his life.

'What are you doing here?' he said when she stood in front of him with a silent smile curving her lips. All he wanted to do was to wrap his hands around her arms and pull her close to him to feel that smile against his own mouth.

'I came to talk to you,' she replied, her breath a bit unsteady. Had she rushed over here?

He dared to grab her by the arm and savoured the lightning shooting through his body at the touch. They weren't even embracing, yet the heat rising in him was as delicious as it was distracting. He knew he couldn't give in to that.

'Talk to me? Sofia, there is nothing left for us to talk about,' he said as he pulled her into a small alleyway just past where the capoeira gym members had set up the *roda*. There were a few stands and people mingling around them, but the noise was less—the air more intimate.

'You don't get to decide that all your own. We were in this together, and I have my opinion on what should happen next. You don't have to agree with it, and my biggest fear is that I've simply misread the situation. That my feelings are a lot deeper than yours.'

Her voice wobbled at the last few words, revealing the effort it took her to speak. Carlos couldn't fight the instinct to comfort her. Didn't want to fight it, either. Because when it came to Sofia, he was finding fewer and fewer reasons within himself to fight what was happening between them. Not when she was putting herself out there for him like this. All she had done, and all she was doing—it had all been for him. He knew that in the depth of his heart, yet she stood in front of him right now, questioning how he felt about her.

'Sofia... You're not...' Carlos paused, searching for words that refused to come. How could he tell her about his feelings for her—when he couldn't give himself to her? Feelings and intentions wrestled inside of him, each one struggling to get the upper hand.

Sofia took a deep breath. 'I see you struggling, and I want to help. I *want* to be the person that you talk to about your struggles, about your fears, about how guilty you feel on the inside. I want to be this person for you, if you let me. Sure, I haven't been through the trauma you have, but I've seen enough in life to empathise with your hurt.'

His heart lurched when she swallowed so hard he could hear it even over the surrounding noise. 'You don't know what it's like to live with this heaviness inside of me. I could never burden you with this and watch it dim your light. You mean too *much* to me for that. Not too little.'

He inhaled sharply in unison with Sofia as the words shot out of his mouth, admitting to the thing he was fighting so hard.

'I do know. Maybe not what it's like to lose

your spouse, but I *do* know what it's like to carry so much guilt around inside yourself. I *do*. And keeping me at arm's length is not going to help you find a way ahead.' She paused, determination burning in her eyes. 'I'm telling you—I know you. I don't need details to know you. You're not someone that's satisfied with patching over holes.'

Her fists clenched at her sides. She pushed her chin out in that gesture of challenge he'd seen every single day since starting at Hospital General de Buenos Aires. She had never once backed down from a fight, letting him know exactly what she thought of him—even now.

Was that what he had been doing? Patching over holes inside of him rather than putting in the effort to properly fix what was broken? It sounded so unlike him, yet he couldn't explain the choices he'd made since that night because he had simply wanted to leave. To leave every reminder of Rosa behind.

'I don't know what to do about this...' The words left him with a heavy breath, and Carlos took a step back, leaning against the wall of the building behind him while staring at his feet.

'You do know. How else would you have taught all of us how to do it? You look at the entire patient, and then you prioritise where to focus first. Carlos...' His name from her lips caused a shower of sparks to trickle through him. Her feet sounded over the worn-out cobblestone as she stepped closer, and then her hands were on his cheeks, pulling him upward until they were looking at each other.

'You're no longer alone in this, *amor*,' she said, her thumbs sweeping over his cheekbones. 'No matter how much you carry around inside you, how much you beat yourself up, I'm not going to freak out and bail. Not on you. I love you.'

The words sent a jolt through him, waking up all his nerve endings and ordering them to go haywire. Something inside him expanded, and he realised it was the spot where Sofia had already made her nest.

For five years, he'd chosen fear. The fear of admitting he'd caused the tragedy that had happened to him. A fear of opening up to people in case they would leave him—or see the things inside of him and run. Fear that sat so deep inside of him, he had welcomed it as his steadfast companion without realising how much it held him back from living his life.

Because choosing fear was easier than confronting it—like Sofia was doing right now. He had pushed her away, choosing his fear of her eventually fading out of his life over the possibility of a lifetime spent with her. But she had chosen differently, had come here to tell him that. To…fight for him.

'I love you, too,' he whispered. As the words left his lips, a weight lifted—unshackled by the admission. Sofia had seen him at his worst, had helped him through his struggle even before they had agreed to their affair. Even now, instead of letting him run away again, she had come to find him.

Her eyes rounded, and she breathed out, 'What?' The grip around his face tightened, her fingers grasping at him as if he could float away any second.

'I'm far from perfect, Sofia. You know that better than anyone else has in the last five years. And you're right. Instead of confronting my problems, I chose to patch over them and run away. A part of me still wants to run.' He wasn't proud to admit that, but he needed to show her *everything* if this was to work. 'I…want to get help. I want to be a better man. For you.'

'Carlos…' Her breath caught in her throat in a small hiccup, and he reached out, wrapping his hands around her waist and pulling her against him. One hand slid into her hair, cupping the back of her neck.

'Thank you for finding me. Again.' Because that's what Sofia had done for him time and again. No matter how hard he'd tried to hide, even from himself, she had found him—and hadn't once retreated from what she'd seen.

He leaned back, pulling her face towards his until their lips met in a kiss that went all the way to his bones.

Carlos had chosen fear for so long, it was hard to fight the instinct. But what wasn't hard was giving his all to the woman softly moaning underneath the press of his lips. She, who had seen him for what and who he was after he had spent the last five years building walls so far and wide that no one would ever dare to even approach him.

For Sofia, he would try anything.

* * * * *

Look out for the next story in the Buenos Aires Docs quartet

Coming soon!

And if you enjoyed this story, check out these other great reads from Luana DaRosa

A Therapy Pup to Reunite Them
The Secret She Kept from Dr. Delgado
The Vet's Convenient Bride

All available now!